My sister is a ghost . . . ?

"If you are here in—" I turned around to face Charlotte Rae and drew my hands up and down. "In . . . in ghost form." My voice cracked. "That means that you were . . ." I swallowed. Hard. "Murdered."

Charlotte Rae stood behind me and looked over my right shoulder at my reflection in the mirror. "I think I put up a fight." She ran her hands down her green skirt, trying to brush the dirt off. She fussed with her messy hair. "Honestly, do you think that I'd look like this if I didn't?"

A tear trickled down my face. My heart was breaking in half. Charlotte Rae and I might've had our differences, but I never wished her dead. Or worse. Murdered.

"Emma Lee Raines, you get yourself together right this minute," Charlotte Rae fussed. "You are tougher than a pine knot. And I don't want to see you grieving over me while I'm here. I want you to get off your keister and find out who killed me and why."

By Tonya Kappes

TONYA KAPPES

A GHOSTLY MORTALITY

A GHOSTLY SOUTHERN MYSTERY

WITNESS
An Imprint of HarperCollinsPublishers

Excerpts from *A Ghostly Undertaking, A Ghostly Grave, A Ghostly Demise, A Ghostly Murder, A Ghostly Reunion* copyright © 2013, 2015, 2017 by Tonya Kappes.

First Witness mass market printing: March 2017

ISBN 978-0-06-246697-6

17 18 19 20 21 QGM 10 9 8 7 6 5 4 3 2 1

Acknowledgments

There are so many people who deserve to be thanked so much! First and foremost, I'm so grateful for Lucia Macro for loving the Southern Ghostly Mystery Series as much as I do.

I have to thank my readers. They keep me going.

I'm grateful for the support of my parents, John Robert and Linda Lowry. Their encouragement for me to follow my dream has given me a life of purpose and meaning.

Thank you to my real-life hero and husband, Eddy Kappes. He takes care of our children and fur babies, not to mention household needs, while he encourages me to escape into my make-believe world.

Prologue

L awdy bee." Granny scooted to the edge of the chair and lifted her arms in the air like she was worshiping in the Sunday morning service at Sleepy Hollow Baptist and the spirit just got put in her.

I sucked in a deep breath, preparing myself for whatever was going to come out of Zula Fae Raines Payne's mouth, my granny. She was a ball of southern spitfire in her five-foot-four-inch frame topped off with bright red hair that I wasn't sure was real or out of a L'Oréal bottle she'd gotten down at the Buy-N-Fly.

"Please, please, please," she begged. "Let me die before anything happens to Emma Lee." Her body slid down the fancy, high-back mahogany leather chair as she fell to her knees with her hands clasped together, bringing them back up in the air as she pleaded to the Big Guy in the sky. "I'm begging you."

"Are you nuts?" My voice faded to a hushed stillness. I glanced back at the closed door of my sister's new office, in fear she was going to walk in and see Granny acting up.

I sat in the other fancy, high-back mahogany leather chair next to Granny's and grabbed her by the loose skin of her underarm. "Get back up on this chair before Charlotte Rae gets back in here and sees you acting like a fool."

"What?" Granny quirked her eyebrows questioningly as if her behavior was normal.

My head dropped along with my jaw in the "are you kidding me" look.

"Well, I ain't lying!" She spat, "I do hope and pray you are the granddaughter that will be doing my funeral, unless you get a flare up of the 'Funeral Trauma.'" She sucked in a deep breath and got up off her knees. She ran her bony fingers down the front of her cream sweater to smooth out any wrinkles so she'd be presentable like a good southern woman, forgetting she was just on her knees begging for mercy.

"Flare up?" I sighed with exasperation. "It's not like arthritis."

The "Funeral Trauma."

It was true. I was diagnosed with the "Funeral Trauma" after a decorative plastic Santa fell off the roof of Artie's Meat and Deli, knocking me flat out cold and now I could see dead people.

I had told Doc Clyde I was having some sort of hallucinations and seeing dead people, but he insisted I had been in the funeral business a little too long and seeing corpses all of my life had brought on the trauma.

Truthfully, the Santa had given me a gift. Not a gift you'd expect Santa to give you, but it was the gift of seeing clients of Eternal Slumber, my family's funeral home business where I was the undertaker. Some family business.

Anyway, a psychic told me I was now a Betweener. I helped people who were stuck between here and the ever after. The Great Beyond. The Big Guy in the sky. One catch . . . the dead people I saw were murdered and they needed me to help them solve their murder before they could cross over.

"I'm fine," I huffed and took the pamphlet off of Charlotte Rae's desk, keeping my gift to myself. The only people who knew were me, the psychic and Sheriff Jack Henry Ross, my hot, hunky and sexy boyfriend. He was as handy as a pocket on a shirt when it came time for me to find a killer when a ghost was following me around. "We are here to get her to sign my papers and talk about this sideboard issue once and for all."

Granny stared at me. My head slid forward like a turtle and I popped my eyes open.

"I'm fine," I said through closed teeth.

"You are not fine." Granny rolled her eyes so big, I swear she probably hurt herself. "People are still going around talking about how you talk to yourself." She shook her finger at me. "If you don't watch it, you are going to be committed. Surrounded by padded walls. Then—" She jabbed her finger on my arm. I swatted her away with the pamphlet. "Charlotte Rae will have full control over my dead body and I don't want someone celebrating a wedding while I lay corpse in the next room. Lawdy bee," Granny griped.

I opened the pamphlet and tried to ignore Granny as best I could.

"Do you hear me, Emma Lee?" Granny asked. I could feel her beady eyes boring into me. "Don't you be disrespecting your elders. I asked you a question," she warned when I didn't immediately answer her question.

"Granny." I placed the brochure in my lap and reminded myself to remain calm. Something I did often when it came to my granny. "I hear you. Don't you worry about a thing. By the time you get ready to die, they will have you in the nuthouse alongside me," I joked, knowing it would get her goat.

The door flung open and the click of Charlotte Rae's high-dollar heels tapped the hardwood floor as she sashayed her way back into her office. The soft linen green suit complemented Charlotte's sparkly green eyes and the chocolate scarf that was neatly tied around her neck. It was the perfect shade of brown to go with her long red hair and pale skin.

"I'm so sorry about that." She stopped next to our chairs and looked between me and Granny. She shook the long, loose curls over her shoulders. "What? What is wrong, now?"

"Granny is all worried I'm going to get sent away to the nuthouse and you are going to lay her out here." The words tumbled out of my mouth before I could stop them. Or did my subconscious take over my mouth? It was always a competition between me and Charlotte, only it was one-sided. Mine.

Charlotte never viewed me as competition because she railroaded me all my life. Like now. She'd left Eternal Slumber with zero guilt, leaving me in charge so she could make more money at Hardgrove's Legacy Center, formerly known as Hardgrove's Funeral Homes until they got too big for their britches and decided to host every life event possible just to make more money.

"I . . ." Granny's mouth opened and then snapped shut. Her face was as red as the hair on her head. "I meant that I didn't want to be placed at Burns Funeral. I don't know what they do down in their morgue."

"Granny." Charlotte Rae eased her toned heinie on the edge of her desk and rested upon it. She planted a smug look on her face. "Here at Hardgrove's, we offer a full line of services. It's the way of the future."

Was she giving us her sales pitch? My jaw clenched. My eyes narrowed. I glared at her perfectly lined hot pink lips. For Charlotte's coloring, she did look great in pink. Heck, she'd look great in a burlap sack. I tucked a strand of my long, dull brown hair behind my ear and folded my hands in my lap with my short bitten-off nails tucked in my palms. She spent a lot of money at the nail salon, getting the perfect manicure, and they did look good.

But today she looked a little tired. Not normal for Charlotte.

"Well, that certainly wasn't the answer I expected to hear." I shook my head. Since Charlotte had left Eternal Slumber Funeral Home, I had forgotten how much of a bossy person she was, until now.

"I'm sorry, Emma Lee." Charlotte crossed her arms over top of her chest. Her brows lifted. Her green eyes lit up a little. "Did I hurt your feel-ings?"

"No." My voice hardened ruthlessly. "But you could at least say that I'm not crazy and for Granny to stop being ridiculous."

I grabbed my purse off the floor and pulled out the envelope full of legal papers I needed Char-lotte to sign to get her out of the family business she had decided to abandon. Not that Hardgrove's Legacy Center was much competition since it was in Lexington, Kentucky.

But it was just like Charlotte to up and leave when times got lean. So lean that I wasn't sure I was going to be able to pay the three employees, other than myself. When clients who had already made pre-need funeral arrangements with Eternal Slumber started pulling out because they didn't want the "Funeral Trauma" girl to handle them in death, Charlotte Rae had jumped ship. She'd taken a job with Hardgrove's at their Lexington location. They had several of these big centers all over Kentucky.

Since they were in Lexington, a good forty min-utes away from Sleepy Hollow, they really weren't our competition. But family was family. And in a small town, family stuck together. Not Char-lotte. She bailed, leaving me with all the chips to pick up. And *that* was exactly what I had done.

Over the past few months, business had doubled and I needed her to sign off on selling her half of the business to me. Plus, I was here about the family sideboard that had been sitting in the foyer of Eternal Slumber for generations. In a moment of weakness years ago, Granny had apparently promised the sideboard to my *dear* sister. Like most of us, I'm sure Granny meant Charlotte Rae could have it after she died. Well, Charlotte was calling for it now. As if she were asking for her inheritance while Granny was alive. Over my dead body.

The sideboard was a beautiful, antique staple in Eternal Slumber and I wasn't about to give it up without a fight or until Granny was six feet under.

I didn't have time to sit here and beg Charlotte to do what was right. I had a Betweener client's funeral to prepare and there was no time to dilly-dally, especially with Charlotte.

"I don't think Granny is being ridiculous. I mean—" Charlotte picked up one of the same brochures I still had in my lap and gave it a good, swift yank. It unfolded like an accordion. "Here at Hardgrove's we are a full-service center." Her pink fingernail pointed to the first photo. "We offer a full line of funeral services with a state-of-the-art facility. Not like the ones in Sleepy Hollow." She referred to our small town of Sleepy

Hollow, Kentucky. And there was the dig about where we grew up.

"You mean Eternal Slumber without saying it?" I wasn't going to let her get away with saying we weren't meeting the needs of our residents.

"No, no." She shook her head and wagged her finger at me like I was some child. "There is also Burns Funeral." She mentioned the only other funeral home in Sleepy Hollow, which was my direct competitor. "They are definitely not top-of-the-line, especially since O'Dell was elected Sleepy Hollow mayor."

"Do tell." Granny lit up like a morning glory; she was tickled pink to hear any and all gossip concerning O'Dell Burns since he beat her in the Sleepy Hollow mayoral election by only two votes.

O'Dell's sister, Bea Allen, had moved back to town to take over the funeral home while O'Dell spent all his time in his plush office at the courthouse.

"This is on the down-low." Charlotte gave the good ole Baptist nod that meant we were supposed to keep our mouths shut because she was about to give us some deep-fried small town gossip, but she obviously forgot she was talking to Granny. "I have had several of Burns's customers come here and change their pre-need funeral arrangements."

Several of Burns's? Her words twirled around in my head like a tornado. The more important question was why on earth would Burns's customers drive all the way to Lexington for a funeral when everyone was in Sleepy Hollow and Eternal Slumber was an option.

"They have?" Granny put her hand to her chest and sucked in. "Who?"

"I'm not going to say, but let me tell you that I heard they put the wrong clothes on the wrong corpse." Charlotte Rae's grin was as big as the Grand Canyon. Granny clapped in delight like a little kid getting a piece of candy, turning my stomach in all sorts of directions at the sight. "Since I know you won't tell"—Charlotte Rae leaned in and whispered—"Old man Ridley died and he was in some sort of the armed services. His family insisted he be buried in his hat. Also, Peggy Wayne was laid out in the room next to old man Ridley and her family wanted to make sure her family pearls were buried with her. When Ridley's widow got there, he had on Peggy Wayne's pearls and Peggy had on Ridley's hat. Ridley's widow jerked the hat off Peggy's ice-cold body, taking her wig off with it."

Granny gasped in horror, only there was a twinkle in her eye of joy that shone greater than a flashlight, encouraging Charlotte Rae to continue her horrid tale.

"Needless to say, it spread all over the gossip

circles and here I am today"—she patted the files behind her on the desk—"working up new contracts."

"Why didn't you send them to Emma Lee?" Granny asked. I was a bit relieved to see she was getting her wits about her.

"I'm not going to turn down business." Charlotte cackled. "I have to make a quota here in order to get my big bonus."

"The Grim Reaper must be busy because Emma Lee's got 'em lined up four dead bodies deep waiting to be buried." Granny was talking way too much. "There's gonna be a lot of good eating coming up, that's for sure."

Although Granny was flapping her jaws way too much, my mouth did water at the thought of the upcoming repass. That was one great thing I loved about our small southern town. Funerals were just as big social gatherings as a wedding. And all the locals put their differences aside to come together, bringing food and giving respect to the deceased. The repass was the meal after the funeral service. And Granny always brought homemade apple or cherry pie. Mmm, mmm, I could taste her buttery crust as if I was eating a piece.

"Is that right, Emma Lee? Business is good?" Charlotte asked, bringing me out of my food dream. There was a trace of surprise on her face.

"Now, Granny." It was time. I put the envelope in front of Charlotte. "Granny is exaggerating." I lied. There were five bodies, not four, and I wasn't going to tell Charlotte Rae that business had picked up until she signed over her half of Eternal Slumber to me. "Here is the paperwork drawn up."

Charlotte Rae took it and carefully lifted the envelope flap. Gingerly she took the papers out and unfolded them, taking a glance at them.

"I'll look them over later." She folded them back up and stuck them back in the envelope.

"Later? How much later?" I demanded to know. "There is nothing in there but you giving up your half of the funeral home. You said you were done and it needs to be final."

"Calm down, Emma Lee." Charlotte patted her palms down to the ground. "I'm going to sign them, but I want to show Granny around before it gets busy in here."

In my head, I jumped up and grabbed Charlotte by her long hair, flung her to the ground—breaking one of her nails of course—and forced her to sign the papers. In reality, I swallowed, grabbed the envelope off her desk and followed her and Granny out of the office.

"Here is where we host some receptions." Charlotte took us into a room filled with round tables and chairs. There was a serving buffet at the front of the room. The room was painted a pale yellow with dark brown crown molding and chair rail. The carpet was maroon with subtle yellow flecks that matched the walls. Pictures on the wall were paintings of retired Keeneland horses that probably cost more than I'll earn in my entire lifetime.

"For the funerals or the weddings?" Granny was getting caught up in the pageantry of the big funeral home center.

"We do not have repasses here at Hardgrove's." Charlotte gestured around the room with her hands like she was one of those models on *The Price Is Right*. "We have a catered chef who prepares fruit trays, cheese plates and small dessert options, along with tea or coffee."

"Why do you need a chef for that?" I questioned, trying to find anything to make Charlotte look bad. "I mean, that's what makes our small town so wonderful." I reminded Charlotte of what she'd left behind. "I think it's comforting how the Auxiliary women put their loving hands in making a special dish for the dearly departed's family and we all come together to share in the family feel of it all."

Charlotte couldn't deny that there was something special about a small town like Sleepy Hollow when it came to a death. Everyone put their differences aside, rallied around each other, supported each other. Not like this big building that seemed so cold and institutional.

Charlotte ignored me and continued telling Granny about how they also used it for wedding receptions along with any other celebration they could think of.

"We have a lot of baby showers too." Charlotte squeezed her shoulders up to her ears in delight. "I just love those."

"Baby showers?" Granny drew back. All five foot four inches of her small frame froze. "Charlotte Rae, didn't we raise you better than that?"

"Granny," Charlotte cackled. "You raised us in a funeral home."

It was true. Charlotte and I were raised in the family living area of the funeral home right alongside Granny. Granny, Momma and Daddy ran the funeral home while Charlotte and I tried to lead a normal life; only, sleeping in a bed in the next room over from a dead body was far from normal. But we managed. Charlotte and I went to mortuary school, my parents retired and Granny retired after she inherited the Sleepy Hollow Inn from her deceased second husband, leaving the funeral home to us.

"Oh, Granny, you raised me fine. Times have changed and so does business." Charlotte pishposhed Granny's comment. She continued to show us around the large building, going on and on about how they had had retirement parties, birthdays and christenings.

"Christenings?" Granny snickered. "You mean to tell me I could go over here to see my dead relative and walk over yonder to see my great-grandbaby get christened all in one day?"

Charlotte ignored Granny and continued on with the grand tour.

"I really would like you to sign these papers." I held the envelope out in front of Charlotte when we walked down the hall to get a look at one of the viewing rooms.

Charlotte skipped around me, not giving any acknowledgment to the papers I practically shoved in her face.

"Shh." Granny batted my hand away and followed right behind Charlotte.

I sucked in a deep breath and tucked a piece of my hair behind my ear, ran my hand down my white T-shirt before I gave in, once again, and followed them to the next room.

The next room looked more like a banquet hall than a viewing room. Large round tables dotting the entire room had crisp baby-blue tablecloths over them and had at least ten chairs around each of them. White taffeta material was stretched and tied around the backs of each chair with a big, stiff bow on the back.

"There you are!" A woman jumped out from behind a large stereo speaker from across the room. And then, lickety-split, she was snapping her fingers and pointing at Charlotte Rae. "My Candy doesn't deserve a fine wedding reception where the flowers smell like those of a funeral!" She put her hands on her hips and turned to me. Her dirty blond hair was clipped short and her black roots were creeping out from her skull. "Can you smell that?" she asked me in a demanding tone. "Death. That is what I smell. And I told my Candy I wasn't going to have a dead body next to my princess as she cut that cake I paid an arm and a leg for. Do you hear me?" She rambled on, not giving Charlotte a chance to even speak.

"I understand." Charlotte Rae tried to calm the woman down.

"No, you don't, or this would not be happening." The woman gave Charlotte a stern look. "This is an outrage and you had better fix it or another one of them rooms will be filled out there!"

"I will take care of it, Melinda." A crimson color crept up the back of Charlotte's neck. In true Charlotte Rae southern charm, she gave Melinda a smile that didn't quite reach her eyes, and said, "I promise, your Candy will have the wedding of her dreams. Which we still have a few weeks for. This is just an example of what the room can look like. The chairs. The linens."

"Her dreams?" Melinda let out a big fit of laughter with a cough. "Hell, she ruined her dreams when she laid down with the Dennis boy. But it ain't no skin off my nose, because I told her I wasn't goin' to raise no more youngin's. Not even my grandbabies."

Granny's eyes darted between Charlotte and Melinda. A delightful grin spread over her face. Charlotte had her hands full and Melinda was giving her a run for her money.

"Momma! You stop talking about us." The shrill voice echoed through the room. A woman who must've been Princess Candy stood in the door-way with a scrawny-looking boy. Candy's black hair was permed to death. She grabbed the boy's hand and bustled over to us, practically dragging him like a rag doll. "She ain't never been happy for me. She's the one who insisted on all this!"

"I also insisted you get that hair dyed back to blond, but you didn't listen to that either." Melinda jerked her head side to side.

"You know my baby doctor said that ain't no good for the baby. All them fumes and all." Candy dropped the boy's hand and stuck her nose up in the air. She took a few quick sniffs. The boy must have been the Dennis boy. Poor guy. I felt sorry for him. He didn't look older than eighteen years old. He was shorter than the princess and he was in desperate need of a haircut, his curls unfurled all over the top of his head.

"You smell that?" Princess Candy smacked the Dennis boy with the backside of her hand before she planted her hands on her hips, causing her baggy shirt to become taut, exposing the outline of what looked to be a pregnant belly. "Death!"

A groan escaped from Charlotte's lips.

"I told you that this place smelled like dead people. Are you trying to piss me off?" Candy came nose to nose with Melinda.

Melinda's arms flew up in the air. "See, I told you!" She pointed to Charlotte and then faced the Dennis boy. "Boy, she's gonna rip your heart right out of you, fry it up and eat it on a biscuit and swallow it down with a big swig of iced tea if you don't run."

"Fix this!" Candy grabbed the boy's hand and flung him toward the door, dragging him all the way out. "Or someone will take the fall for this!"

"Fix what?" Gina Marie Hardgrove, owner of Hardgrove's Funeral Homes, walked into the event room carrying a tray of glasses filled with sweet tea and finger sandwiches, dodging the lovebirds. "Oh my!" Gina placed the tray on the table before she gave Granny a hug. "Zula, it's been so long." She held Granny out at arm's length, getting a good look at her. I couldn't stop looking at that big, baseball-sized diamond on her finger. "You haven't changed a bit. And this one." Gina let go of Granny and patted Charlotte on the back. "She is such an asset to Hardgrove's. I really am sorry we stole her from you." She gave me a wink.

In the south, a wink speaks volumes and Gina Marie's wink was more of a dig than a compliment. Memories of Gina Marie flooded over me.

As kids, we'd see the Hardgrove family at different funeral conventions and all us kids would hang out together. Then there had been mortuary school. Gina Marie was there with me and Charlotte. That damn ring of hers was why I got a C minus in the class. I spent most of my days dreaming of having one. The Hardgroves had several funeral homes across the state of Kentucky to our one.

"Now I can go and visit our other centers, knowing I'm leaving here with our Lexington center in good hands." Gina Marie nodded over to Charlotte who had gingerly taken Melinda aside and talked to her in the corner of the room.

"I guess we better go." Granny tugged on my arm.

"When you get a moment, can you please have

Charlotte sign the papers?" I handed them to Gina Marie.

"She still hasn't signed these?" Her face turned white and a scowl swept over her nose. "She did sign a non-compete with us, so I'm going to have to take this up with her."

Charlotte left Melinda in the corner and joined us, jerking the envelope from Gina Marie's hand. "It has nothing to do with a non-compete," she assured Gina Marie before turning toward me and Granny and gesturing for us to get the heck out of there.

A small stab hit my heart as Charlotte Rae quickly recovered from the embarrassing scene with a warm smile. Something I was never able to compete with.

"It was so good of you to come by. Emma Lee, I'll get these back to you soon." She waved the envelope in the air with one hand and shooed us out the sliding front door with the other. "I must get back to work. Unlike Eternal Slumber, we are always busy with a life event. Yoo-hoo, Arley!" Charlotte raced over to one of the gardens in the front of the funeral home. "You need to put the ducklings in the fountain!"

There was no reason to fuss with her because she wasn't going to listen and Granny had already started off toward the car. I recognized Arley Burgin, Hardgrove's grave digger and evidently lawn boy, standing in the fountain with bright yellow gloves clear up to his elbow and a scrub brush in one of his hands. I didn't know Arley all that well, but he was on the men's softball team that was sponsored by Eternal Slumber. He had mentioned he wasn't a fan of Gina Marie which tickled me pink, and by the look on his face, he wasn't a big fan of Charlotte's either.

"Y'all a new client here at Hardgrove's?" The security guard gave me and Granny the once-over after he moseyed up to us.

"No." I pointed to our car, a hearse, which should've been a pretty good indicator to him that we were in the same business. "I'm Charlotte's sister and this here is our granny. We are from Sleepy Hollow."

"Burns?" he questioned.

"Why, I never," Granny gasped and glared. "Do we look like we come from them good-for-nothin' . . ."

"Eternal Slumber," I chirped up and cut Granny off. "Have a nice day. Get into the car, Granny." My brows lifted.

"I knew I should've drove the 'ped." Granny referred to the moped she drove around town. She huffed, got in the car and slammed the door.

I looked at the security guard and rolled my eyes so hard that I thought I hurt myself.

"Oh my stars." Granny buckled up. "That was a sight for sore eyes."

I started the engine and pretended to adjust the rearview mirror when I was really looking back at Charlotte. It was good southern manners to stand outside and wave bye as someone pulled off in their car, but bad luck to watch them completely drive off. When we were almost out of sight, Charlotte stomped her feet and hurried back into Hardgrove's.

"I'm a little disappointed in how she reacted to that nasty woman." Granny sat poised with her hands in her lap. "She should've told her that there were a few funerals being held and the flowers would be removed way before the wedding." Granny lifted her hand and nervously tapped her finger on the door handle. "Who on earth ever heard of opening a place like that?"

"Really?" I gripped the wheel, turning on the road that took us right back home to Sleepy Hollow where we belonged. "The fact that she hasn't signed the paperwork should be what you can't believe. I mean, she's working illegally for Gina Marie."

"Pish-posh." Granny brushed me off. "She's not happy there. I can see it in her eyes. It's just a matter of time before she comes back to Eternal Slumber. Mark my words, that is why she hasn't signed those papers."

And that was my fear.

Chapter 1

In no time and with a little bit of a lead foot, I had the hearse parked in the back of Eternal Slumber. It was still strange not seeing Charlotte's car parked in the space right up against the back door, because Lord forbid she walk any farther than she needed to. Charlotte had always claimed that since she was the one who "sold" our packages that she needed to be presentable, which meant the less she did to mess herself up, the better.

While Charlotte was here, I was in charge of making sure the arrangements for the family were carried out as they had planned, the burial service was ready and all the details were taken care of, like the repass, flowers, memory cards and any other details.

"I better get out of here." Granny opened the door and grabbed her black leather touring helmet off the seat next to her and strapped it under her chin. "I left Hettie in charge and God only knows what concoction she made at the juice bar. Plus, I still have to make my pies for dinner tonight."

Hettie Bell owned Pose and Relax, the yoga studio next to Eternal Slumber. She also helped Granny on a part-time basis at the Sleepy Hollow Inn when Granny needed someone. Hettie was a health nut and would make up all sorts of lime-green, slimy drinks to serve to the customers when Granny was gone. Hettie said that the tourists who visited our town for our famous caves needed to be in tip-top shape for them to hike and spelunk. Granny always lifted a brow when Hettie went on with her herbal mumbo jumbo. I simply smiled.

"Don't you be worrying about nothing." Granny slipped the aviator goggles over her eyes, instantly magnifying them three times their normal size. "It'll all work out the way it's supposed to."

"That's an upbeat attitude, Granny." I smiled and got out of the hearse, slamming the door behind me.

"Mm, hmm." Granny groaned. She bent down and unlocked the padlock she used to lock the chain around the tree and her moped. Granny was worried about someone stealing her ride. She carried a heavy-duty chain to secure her moped to anything that was bolted down. You couldn't get anything more bolted into the ground than a tree. Granny threw her leg over her moped.

"Between me and you"—Granny flipped the switch and twisted the moped handle to full throttle—"she's lost her ever-loving mind working for them Hardgroves. Mark my words, she's gonna regret it. Do you need any help with Jade?" Granny nodded toward the line of television network vans that had parked along the curve of the town square.

Granny referred to Jade Lee Peel, my current client at Eternal Slumber. Her funeral was late this afternoon. Jade was sort of a celebrity from Sleepy Hollow. She'd been in town for a class reunion and had used the opportunity to launch her new reality TV show about her. She'd left Sleepy Hollow after high school to pursue her modeling and acting career. I'm not going to lie—I might stretch the truth a tad, but I didn't lie—Jade and I weren't the best of friends and she wasn't the nicest of classmates. In fact, she was the one who had given me the name Creepy Funeral Home Girl. Needless to say she crossed one too many people and found herself on the other side of the ground. Six feet under. It just so happened that

Eternal Slumber was hosting her funeral, and the tabloid television shows were all over it.

"I'm good. I've got it all covered." I grinned through my big lie. When I'd left this morning, Mary Anna Hardy, Eternal Slumber beautician and owner of Girl's Best Friend Spa, had yet to get Jade's makeup on.

In one motion, Granny pulled her wrist back, planted her feet on the footrest and whizzed out of the parking lot. The only thing I could do was shake my head. There was no way I was ever going to get over seeing my seventy-seven-year-old granny driving a moped for transportation when she'd had a perfectly nice car before she decided to trade it in for the hunk of junk.

"I thought I heard you pull in." Vernon Baxter stood on the small porch at the back entrance of the funeral home. He was a stately-looking older man with white hair sprinkled with dark. He was a very handsome man. He was not only the county coroner, but he did all the stuff I didn't like to do. The embalming.

It took a special person to cut open a dead body, take out all of their organs and drain their fluids. Of course I was trained in embalming, but if I could pay someone else to do it, it was better for me.

"The phone has been ringing off the hook and I took several messages from the families we have lined up." He held out a bunch of square Post-it notes. "Artie Peel wants to know what time they need to be here for the final viewing."

Before the funeral, I always scheduled a time where the deceased's loved ones had time to give their final goodbyes. Artie was a beloved member of the community and owner of Artie's Meat and Deli. It was a shame what had happened to Jade. She was his only daughter. Plus his wife had died when Jade was young.

"What is it about winter to spring?" I asked and walked up the steps, taking the notes from him. He opened the door and held it for me.

"I guess death is just like the seasons. Winter kills things and spring brings life." He followed me into the back of the funeral home where the employee kitchen was located.

"Whoa!" I jumped to the side when I felt something brush up against my leg and race into the funeral home. "What was that?" I asked and looked inside.

"What?" Vernon asked with a whistle of surprise. He looked around to see what I was all jumpy about.

"I'm not going in there until you see what that was." Sleepy Hollow was set in the foothills of Kentucky and the caves were a backdrop to our town. Many critters lived in these parts and you just never knew what was going to show up. "Some sort of vermin ran in the back door. It could've been a po-cat or a possum because I felt its tail rub my leg."

"I didn't see anything. And I certainly don't smell anything." Vernon lifted his nose in the air. Both of those critters did have distinct smells.

He looked around while I stood outside.

"Nothing." He poked his head back out the door. "The kitchen door is even closed off to the rest of the building, so maybe it was the wind."

"Maybe." I looked behind me at the tree line behind the funeral home. Not a single leaf was blowing. There was no wind. I bent down and rubbed my calf thinking it might've been a leg spasm, so I put the incident behind me and walked in the funeral home.

When I was growing up, the entire back of the funeral home was our family home. Charlotte and I shared a bedroom, Granny had her own and so did my parents. There was a family room where we watched television and a kitchen, along with a couple of bathrooms. After Charlotte and I took over, we knew it was time to remodel and update. Since Charlotte had her own apartment, I decided to stay. We transformed the living quarters into another viewing room, but kept part of the kitchen for the employees. We kept our bedroom and turned Granny's room into a little kitchenette and TV room for me. Since it was only me, I didn't need a lot of space. There was a separate entrance also in the back for my small apartment. It was plenty big for me.

"Thank you for taking the calls. And making some coffee." I walked over to the freshly brewed pot of coffee and poured some in a mug. "It's exactly what I need to calm my nerves after fussing with Charlotte."

"How was she?" Vernon asked.

It had come as a big shock to everyone when she left us and moved out of Sleepy Hollow. It was almost a scandal when she left. The town gossips were all abuzz with speculation as to why she left for another funeral home. But we just kept our heads high and said it was a better opportunity for her.

Granny took it harder than anyone. She felt betrayed by Charlotte Rae. It was apparent from Granny's comments earlier.

"I don't know." I blew on the much-needed coffee and let the steam swirl up before I took a sip. "You know Charlotte. She makes everything look as if it was all coming up roses. But Granny"—I shook my head—"she still isn't over Charlotte leaving. I felt bad for her today when Charlotte paraded us around that building showing us how she hosts wedding receptions, baby showers—"

"Baby showers?" Vernon's head jerked back and he looked at me as if I had two heads.

"Yep. I've never seen anything like it. Charlotte is not only a funeral director, she's a party planner now." I laughed.

"Did you get the papers signed?" Vernon asked.

Vernon was not only my employee, he had become like a father figure to me, and since Charlotte left, I found I went to Vernon for business advice.

"Nope." I filled my mug again and shuffled through the Post-it notes, taking a look to see who had called. I leaned my hip on the edge of the counter and looked at Vernon. "That is one thing I don't get. If she's so happy, then why not sign the papers?"

"Maybe she's having second thoughts." Vernon shrugged. "I've got to get back to Jade and sign off on her papers to give to Jack Henry."

"You're all finished?" I asked knowing he'd have to get his final autopsy report to Jack Henry Ross, Sleepy Hollow sheriff and my hunky boy-friend.

"Mary Anna had come to do Jade's makeup but I still had to sew Jade's eyes shut." Vernon made a sewing motion with his hand, sending chills up my spine. "Mary Anna is down there now shining up the tiara."

The tiara was a perfect touch to Jade's final resting place. I'd even gotten a horse from Dottie Kramer so Jade's coffin could be pulled to the cemetery in a horse-drawn carriage. My only problem was finding a Cinderella-style carriage. Another reason why Charlotte had left a bad taste in my mouth. She'd come down here after word that Jade Lee Peel had died and tried to get Artie to use Hardgrove Legacy Center to lay Jade to rest. She'd even promised a Cinderella-style carriage. I promised it too, just to nail down Jade's funeral here. Unfortunately, I wasn't having any luck finding a carriage.

"Thanks, Vernon." It was nice to not have to worry about going down the checklist like I used to have to do with Charlotte Rae. "At least we know Jade would've loved this hullabaloo." I pointed to the door because Jade would've loved all the attention from the news media.

Before Charlotte had left with less than a twenty-four-hour notice, I had a checklist of sorts. Vernon would tell Charlotte when the body was ready to be dressed and Charlotte would call Mary Anna Hardy.

I couldn't do my own hair and makeup, much less the dead's. Not Mary Anna. She said she liked working on the corpses better than her living clients because they didn't talk back to her or complain.

Still, Charlotte was in charge of all of that. After the family viewed the body, it was my turn to take over and Charlotte moved on to the next family. I made sure the funeral went smoothly and the parlor was ready for viewing. Charlotte didn't like to attend the funeral part. She said she didn't like to see people cry and act all sad. Who did? Since Charlotte refused to do it, lucky me, I had to deal with it.

Now that I was in charge, it seemed like everything ran a little smoother since I wasn't a micromanager like Charlotte. Vernon knew the drill and he and I worked like a finely oiled machine. Instead of giving me the burden of calling Mary Anna, he took it on as part of his duties to leave out the middle man and call her himself. That way if there was some sort of special fill-in, like a little more putty on the nose area or an abnormality Mary Anna could cover up with makeup, he could tell her himself. So far so good.

"I'll go ahead and call Artie." I did a quick check of the time by pulling my cell out of my back pocket. "I'll make sure to get the front viewing room ready for him because Sissy Phillips's family requested the east room because that was where her daddy was laid out." Sissy's funeral was in the morning and I was sure Vernon hadn't even started on her yet. It was going to be a late night for all of us here at Eternal Slumber.

It wasn't uncommon for a family to request a certain viewing room especially if they had used it before. Whatever made them comfortable was fine with me. It was hard enough to lose a family member, so I tried to make the funeral planning a little easier on them. It was nice when the deceased had pre-need arrangements because then there was no decision-making needed from the grieving family. All the decisions had been made. But with Charlotte gone, I was finding it hard to do everything. Even if she was having second thoughts, I would never admit life had been much easier with her here. Or to clarify, life was a little easier when I had an extra set of hands . . . not necessarily her perfectly manicured ones because she never got down into the nitty-gritty.

Vernon got on the elevator and I walked into my office, the one that used to be Charlotte's. It was much larger than the one I used to have and furnished much nicer. It was where the family would come to sign all the final papers, so we made sure it was a comfortable and welcoming space for them.

Death was such a sad and final experience that

I tried to make it as nice as I could. I grabbed the portable phone off the charger that sat on the credenza behind the desk and plopped down on the cream leather couch in front of the window while I dialed Jack Henry.

"Good morning." I couldn't stop the smile that automatically found a place on my face when I heard Jack Henry's voice answer. I sank deeper into the large pillows Charlotte used as decoration only and let my body melt as I talked to him. "I wanted to call and hear a happy voice before I call back my clients and get ready for Jade's funeral."

It was true. Jack Henry made me feel so warm and fuzzy inside that calling him first thing in the morning before returning the calls from my clients really helped me and was becoming part of my routine.

Knowing I had a lot of work left to do, I got up and walked down the hall into the vestibule of the funeral home before taking a right into the viewing room. The chairs were set up for Jade's funeral, but I still needed to finish putting the slipcovers over some of them.

"Good morning. I was going to stop by, but when I drove by, I saw your hearse was gone and Zula's moped chained to the tree. I knew you must've gotten your courage up to go see Charlotte." Jack's deep southern drawl melted my heart. It took everything I had not to throw in the towel for the day and spend it with him. Especially now that I only had me to answer to. "How was it? Did she sign the papers?"

"It was weird and no, she didn't." I groaned and walked over to the storage room door. Every viewing room had their own storage room filled with linens for the funerals and other items like Kleenex and floral stands.

I barely got the door open when the orange-and-white-striped tail darted inside.

"Oh my." Quickly, I slammed the door shut. I knew something brushed up against my leg and now that I'd seen the tail, I would bet money it was a feral cat, which wouldn't be uncommon in our wooded area. "I knew I felt something earlier."

"Huh?" Jack Henry sounded confused.

"I think a feral cat got into the funeral home."

"A cat?" Jack asked.

"Yes," I whispered and slightly opened the door with my eye looking through the crack.

A flash of orange whipped past me. I jumped around to face the chairs, and the tail danced around and under them. I walked down the aisle with my phone pinned between my ear and shoulder, looking all around the room to see if I could find the cat. The last thing we needed was the Peel family to come in here and a cat appear out of nowhere.

"Didn't a cat get in there once before?" Jack Henry asked, reminding me of a very bad situation that I had wanted to forget.

"Umhmm." I bent down and looked underneath the chairs. A long time ago I had secretly kept a cat in my bedroom. Charlotte Rae had left my door open and the cat got out when there was a funeral going on. During Pastor Brown's final prayer when everyone's head was bowed, the cat had apparently jumped in the casket and curled up right on the funeral pillow. When everyone opened their eyes, screams came from all directions. Needless to say, we'd lost a couple of clients after that and it had spread all over town about how Eternal Slumber let feral animals into the funeral home. Business might've recovered after a few months, but the gossip never did stop and still to this day the cat incident was occasionally brought up.

"I don't see that cat." I stood up and looked around, scratching my head.

"You actually saw a cat?" Jack asked.

"I saw a cat tail in the air." I knew I sounded crazy, but I'd seen many more things that others couldn't. "Anyways, Charlotte kind of pushed the papers aside like it was no big deal and told me she would get to it later." I opened the door of the storage room and flipped on the light. "And I mentioned it to Gina Marie Hardgrove. She was mad because Charlotte hadn't signed them."

"Why would that be skin off her back?" Jack asked.

"Apparently Charlotte signed a non-compete with them." My eyes scanned the room for a roaming tail.

"That doesn't make sense since Eternal Slumber is nowhere near Hardgrove's." He made a good point.

"Charlotte did say that she was getting some of Burns's clients, which still makes no sense to me since I'm right here." I let out an exasperated, long sigh and walked back over to the storage closet to get a few more slipcovers. I might as well get something done while I was on the phone.

"Here, kitty, kitty," I bent down and tried to see if the cat had made its way back into the closet and squeezed underneath the lowest shelf. I didn't know a thing about cats, but I did know they could work their way into tight spaces.

I didn't know much about animals in general. My parents didn't allow animals in our home—the cat in the coffin is a good example of why.

"You see the cat?" Jack Henry's voice escalated. Our conversation had turned back to the cat.

"I think a cat went back in the storage room." I got on my hands and knees and continued to crawl around looking in all the tight spaces. "Did you hear me say Charlotte said she'd sign them later?"

"How much later?" Jack asked a good question. "She's been gone for months now."

"Granny seems to think Charlotte is regretting her decision." I wouldn't bother telling Jack Henry all the details of my visit to Hardgrove's. Although my sister and I didn't get along that well, we were still sisters and I didn't want to make her look any more stupid than Melinda and her daughter had made her look earlier in the day. Even if it was only gossip between me and Jack Henry, it was still gossip.

"Do you think she is?" Jack asked.

"I don't know, but maybe I'll go back out to see her without Granny," I suggested and stood back up. There was no hide nor hair of the cat to be seen.

I grabbed the blue linen chair covers off the shelf. Artie had picked out a blue sparkly pageant dress of Jade's to lay her to rest. It would definitely look very Cinderella-ish.

"That would probably be a good idea. Say, I've got some free time for lunch before the funeral. Do you want to meet at the inn for lunch?" he offered.

"That sounds great." I hated to pass up any time I could spend with Jack Henry. "But I still need to find a carriage for the funeral." I was starting to regret making a promise to Artie about the carriage when I had no idea where or how to get one. I'd called many places that rent those types of things for sweet sixteen birthdays and parades, but no one had returned my calls.

Really I wanted to run back up to see Charlotte before Jade's funeral and talk to her myself. I didn't want anyone to know, not even Jack.

"So I won't see you until the funeral?" he asked with a touch of disappointment in his tone.

Sleepy Hollow shut down when there was a funeral. Jack Henry always led the funeral procession in his cruiser. I didn't know what it was about those lights, but when he turned them on, he turned me on.

"We can make up for lost time after the funeral." I looked down at my watch and bit my lip, wondering how I was going to fit Jack Henry in my nightly plans since Sissy was a top priority. There was no way I was going to tell Jack Henry that.

"Is that a promise?"

"If I'm lying, I'm dying." I shut my eyes so tight they almost hurt. I was preparing myself to get struck down by lightning. I had made a promise to Jack that I wasn't sure I was going to be able to keep.

I had a couple of hours to get everything set up for Sissy in the other room. The memory books for both Sissy and Jade had been sent to Fluggie Callahan, and I needed to return the calls before I could head back to Hardgrove's. I was going to get Charlotte alone one way or another.

"Did you find the cat?" Jack Henry asked.

"No, but I'll tell John Howard to keep an eye out for it. See you soon." I hit End and added a couple of blue casket drapes to my growing pile.

"Hell fire! Where is everyone?" I heard someone yell from the viewing room. "I know someone's got to be here," the voice grumbled.

I walked out of the closet and put the linens on one of the folded chairs.

"Honey, I was beginning to wonder what was going on around here." Marla Maria Teater stood in the middle of the room with the biggest casket spray of blue carnations I had ever seen. She wore a bright pink jumpsuit that zipped up the front, but stopped in the middle of her cleavage. A dog leash was fastened around her wrist and the other end was attached to Lady Cluckington, Marla Maria's prize Orloff pet hen.

"What on earth are you doing?" I asked, taking a good look at the flowers.

A white sash across the arrangement read *Daughter, Friend, Queen*.

"Are you okay?" Marla took one good look at me and dropped the flower spray on the floor.

When she rushed over, the leash dropped and Lady pecked the flowers. Marla ignored her and used the pads of her fingers to tap underneath my eyes.

"You haven't been using the Preparation H I gave you." She grabbed my chin with her fingers, giving it a good jerk side to side and up and down. "I don't go around wasting beauty tips on just no one. I expected you, of all my girls, to take my advice."

"I appreciate all of your advice." I jerked my head back and out of her pinchers. I rubbed my chin, feeling the indentions of the nails she'd embedded in me. She was right. I hadn't done much about my appearance because I was busy.

I stared at her for a second, wondering if she remembered that it was dead people that were my clients and they for sure didn't care if I had bags, circles or even wrinkles around my eyes.

"Advice?" She ran her hands down my hair and fluffed up a few of the layers. "Preparation H is not advice, it's a miracle for those little wrinkles under your eyes." She tapped my eyes again. She sucked her lips in real tight. "If it can shrink a hemorrhoid, think about those wrinkles. And you have a hot cop to keep on the line." Her puckered lips disturbed me on so many levels.

I put my hand on my heart. "I will use it tonight. I promise." I looked back down at the flowers, closed my eyes and gulped. That would be two promises I probably wasn't going to be able to keep.

"If you don't start taking care of yourself, you are going to be right up there." She lifted her arm and pointed to the front of the viewing room.

"Now, what are you doing here with that?" I had to change the subject. I might be in the business of death, but I didn't want to think about my own.

"Oh no." Marla Maria's face melted into a frown. Lady had given that funeral flower spray a run through the ringer. "If Dottie Kramer knew I dropped this on the floor, she'd skin my hide and pluck off all of Lady's gorgeous feathers for getting a hold of it."

"Dottie Kramer?" I asked.

"You haven't heard?" Marla Maria was bent over the flower arrangement, plucking and picking off the stems that had bent, broke and been nibbled on. "Dottie Kramer opened up a florist in her barn. She has done so well with her vegetables, she decided to try out her green thumb. And she dropped off that old humpback horse you wanted for Jade's carriage."

I went behind her and picked up the pieces she discarded. "And you are helping her?"

"When I was at Artie's delivering the eggs, she was in there sticking all sorts of fresh flowers in buckets of water near the register. Artie said he'd let her give it a go and my goodness, they were all gone by the end of the morning rush."

"You still deliver eggs to Artie's?" I was stuck on the fact she continued her deceased husband's job because, when he was alive, she'd complained to high heavens. She nodded. "I bet Chicken is real happy about that."

I referred to her deceased husband, Chicken Teater. Murdered husband. In fact, Chicken was the second Betweener client that had come to me because he was murdered. I'm not going to lie, I had thought Marla Maria killed him because she was jealous of Lady Cluckington, but after putting my amateur sleuthing skills to the test and sticking my nose in places it shouldn't have been stuck in, I did find out who killed him and why.

"It just seemed fittin' since Chicken did a good job at it, and what in hell am I going to do with all of them eggs?" Marla Maria stood up and brushed her hands together before she picked up Lady's leash and wrapped it back around her wrist. "Now, where is Jade?"

It wouldn't be unusual for Marla Maria to ask to see Jade. Marla Maria also ran the pageant school on the outskirts of town for young women who wanted to be beauty queens. She had been fascinated with Jade Lee Peel.

"She won't be out until this afternoon, but I'll be sure to put those in the refrigerator and place them right on top of her big blue casket." I didn't want to risk the media getting a photo of Jade like the many they'd done of celebrities in their caskets. I walked over to the linens and picked the top one up and snapped it open. "You didn't answer my question—are you helping Dottie?"

I had just been to Marla's pageant school and it was packed. It would seem strange for her to spend time working for Dottie when the school was doing so well.

"Just on funeral arrangements. You know I'm

busy with the pageant school." Marla Maria had used the big plot of land Chicken left her in his will to open the beauty pageant school.

Pageantry was taken just as seriously as horse racing around these parts and if anyone could make a business out of teaching girls how to walk, talk and bow, it was former Miss Kentucky, Marla Maria Teater.

"I don't know much about dead people and it really gives me the goose bumps being in here, so I'm sorry if you need help since Charlotte left, but I don't think I can help out." Marla brushed her hands down her jumpsuit and folded them at her waist.

"I'm good." I smiled. "I don't need help."

"From what I heard, you and Zula hightailed it out of town this morning to go see Charlotte." Marla was fishing for information. "I mean, I overheard something like that."

"Spill it."

"Oh, honey." Marla foo-foo'ed me with her hand. "Don't be getting your panties in a bind. It was just girl talk. You know how those Auxiliary women can be when nothing else is going on in town." She turned and trotted toward the vestibule. She called over her shoulder, "They don't have nothing better to talk about." Her fingers drummed the air. "Toodles!"

Chapter 2

Thank goodness I worked well under pressure because I got Jade Lee's viewing room done in record time. She would've loved it. Fluggie Callahan called to say that she'd come by a bit before the visitation so she could drop the memorial cards on her way to drop off the weekly newspapers to the stores. Fluggie was the owner and editor of the *Sleepy Hollow Gazette*, the only paper in town.

I had even gotten some of Sissy Phillips's viewing room ready. Not completely, but some, which would let me have a little more time with Jack Henry instead of spending all night with poor Sissy before we stuck her six feet under. I had a couple hours left before I had to open the doors for Artie to view Jade. Mary Anna had assured me Jade would be fixed up and in front of the viewing room window long before that time, allowing me to jump in the hearse and pay Charlotte a quick visit without Granny.

The fountain Arley had been working on earlier at Hardgrove's was spewing bright pink water out of its jets. He was running around chasing after a cygnet, a baby swan. The closer he got, the more it flapped and squalled. He glanced my way. His arm lifted and he swiped it across the sweat that had beaded up on his forehead.

I put the car in Park, smiled and waved. He groaned and dove for the resting cygnet, catching it in his grips. He held it high in the sky, pumping his hands in the air like he had just made the final winning shot at the NCAA basketball championship game.

I shook my head and got out of the hearse. There were a few more cars in the parking lot and I was happy to see Charlotte's was still there. When I walked in, I could hear some voices. Loud voices. And one of them was Charlotte's.

I walked in the direction of the echoing and escalating voices, stopping briefly when I noticed a painting on the wall that I hadn't notice earlier. It was of Gina Marie Hardgrove and her two brothers. My stomach churned as I read the gold plaque:

Hardgrove Family. It brought back the memories of those two boys following Charlotte around like lovesick puppies at some of the conventions our parents had taken us to.

No wonder Gina Marie was the one to take over. Her brothers were too busy trying to mark Charlotte Rae as their property, telling her they were going to be the Funeral Kings of Kentucky and she could be the queen. They'd fed her lines that she could get a big ring like Gina. Maybe that was what had been in Charlotte's head when we took over Eternal Slumber, but then she realized we were just a small town, homegrown funeral home and we really did just care about comforting the family in a time of need. I couldn't help but wonder if she figured out we weren't going to make the money she needed for the life she wanted.

"Listen here, Charlotte," Gina Marie spit out. "You better find that donation card because I am not going to make another insurance claim on your behalf. This is awfully suspicious."

Donation cards were not uncommon in the undertaker industry. Most of the time, the family would donate the deceased's clothes or housing items the family didn't want. Most funeral homes provided a donation card so the family didn't have to worry about all the tedious things.

"I'm telling you that I put the card in the file before they closed the casket." Charlotte's voice quivered. A tone I had never heard from her. "Ask Sammy."

"Maybe that is your problem. You are spending too much time with my brother on Hardgrove time and forgetting to finish the paperwork."

My ears perked up.

"Sammy is married. He is off-limits. You have had your eye on him since you paraded around those conventions. When I hired you, I told him to stay far away from this location. And now he tells me he is leaving his wife, which will put a piece of Hardgrove's hard-earned dollars in her hands. Something I cannot let happen. Does this have anything to do with you? Because I swear if it does, you'll regret it! Plus, you need to sign off on those papers your crazy sister was flapping her lips about because you are in breach of contract."

That was it! It was bad enough she insulted Charlotte Rae by thinking Charlotte would lay down with that dog, Sammy Hardgrove, but to call me crazy. *I'll show her crazy.*

"Come on in, look around." I bolted in Charlotte Rae's office and talked to the empty space next to me like someone was there. "Can you believe this? Charlotte Rae has moved up in the world. And you can stay here with her." I let out a crazy cackle in the air. My mouth slammed shut and my eyes grew big like I was nuts. "Oops. Did I just say that out loud?" I rolled my finger around my ear. "Forgive me, I have the 'Funeral Trauma' and I forgot to take my little pill from Doc Clyde."

If Gina Marie was going to call me crazy, I was going to embrace it and parade it around.

"Emma, what are you doing back here?" Charlotte Rae's eyes were red around the rim, matching her hair. I stood there like a good crazy girl and looked between her and Gina. "I'm sorry, Gina. Can I have a few minutes with my sister?"

"Make it fast or you will be riding back to Sleepy Hollow in that broke-down hearse with her." Gina flipped around and stomped out of the room.

"What a biiitch," I groaned when the door was safely shut behind me.

"Shut up, Emma," Charlotte whispered, rushing over to the shut door and putting her ear up. "She's out there listening," she mouthed, pointing to the door.

"Sammy? Sammy Hardgrove?" I asked when she gave me the thumbs-up to talk freely. "Seriously? He's so crooked, you can't tell by his tracks if he's coming or going."

"No one knows." She shrugged and wiped the tears from her face. "I thought no one knew." She shook her head and walked over to the window. She crossed her arms and stared out the window. "I just think I need time to adjust."

"Time to adjust? You have been here a few months and I really need for you to sign those papers." The envelope was still sitting on her desk. I picked them up and walked over to her. I held them out. "Charlotte. Why are you pushing back on me over a decision you made? It's been like this all our lives. You always put your needs first and I let you. I'm done with this. Sign the papers."

"I will." Charlotte growled and she jerked the envelope out of my hand and ripped it in half, throwing it on the ground.

"Oh my God, Charlotte, you deserve everything this nasty place does to you! You are dumber than a bag full of hammers." I shook my head. "Granny will die when I tell her about this!" I bent down and picked up the ripped-in-half envelope. "You will hear from my lawyer!"

"Lawyer?" Slowly she turned around, and a devilish look came into her eyes. "You mean Ruby Rose, who got his degree online?" An evil laugh escaped her. "Besides, Sammy loves me. He has always loved me. And he is going to prove it."

"People think I'm crazy? Boy, do they have the wrong sister!" I jerked the door handle open and stomped out.

I couldn't help but notice Gina Marie was consoling a woman in one of the fancy sitting rooms. I curled my fist and crunched the envelope in my grasp. Even though I was mad at Charlotte, Gina Marie talking to her like that didn't sit well in my soul. I wasn't sure who I was mad at more: Charlotte Rae or Gina Marie.

Either way, I didn't have any more time to devote to Charlotte Rae. She'd taken up way too much of my time and I had a funeral to put on.

On the way back into Sleepy Hollow I planned on making a pit stop at the cemetery to make sure John Howard Lloyd, my grave digger—among many other hats he wore around the funeral home—had dug the hole an extra foot. Artie insisted Jade be buried at least seven feet under the earth instead of six. Something about if it ever flooded, which to my knowledge had never happened in Sleepy Hollow.

He had bought plots next to each other in the newer part of the cemetery where I had marked a plot off for me and Charlotte Rae. Was Charlotte planning on changing her pre-need arrangements, I wondered as the hearse took the curves back to Sleepy Hollow. Surely to goodness Hardgrove's had some sort of employee plan like we did. Why would Charlotte want to be buried without family around? Then again, why wouldn't she? All of our people laid in peaceful rest at Sleepy Hollow Cemetery.

The sign for the Buy-N-Fly off in the distance made my taste buds tingle for a Big Gulp Diet Coke. I jerked the hearse a hard right into the parking lot, barely missing Everett Atwood, who was pumping gas, and completely missed hitting the orange-and-white-striped tabby cat that had run out in front of me. Everett wrenched back, and the gas nozzle sprayed gas all over Beulah Paige Bellefry's bright red Cadillac. My face scrunched up and an audible groan escaped me.

"Emma Lee Raines!" Beulah Paige spat out of her pink lips. She lifted her fist in the air and ran over to me. She beat that fist on my window. "Are you crazy? That gas better wipe off and not take the paint off my car or Eternal Slumber will be buying me a brand-new Caddy!" She stuck her fist in the air.

"Did you want me to kill the cat that ran right in front of me?" I pointed in the direction where the feline I had swerved to miss had run off. I wasn't in the business of burying animals. And I wasn't going to start today. I got out of the car, ready to take my punishment from her.

"You can bet your boots I'm going to document

this!" She huffed and puffed up like a blowfish. Her fake lashes batted against her fake tan. She was the only woman I knew who stayed tan all year around and kept her hair as apple red as Granny's. Her bright blue eyes pierced me.

I tapped on her pocketbook that swung from the crook of her arm. "I bet you have a journal in there all about me, don't you?"

"You are crazy!" Beulah jerked the purse closer to her body. "Emma Lee! No wonder your sister left you high and dry."

She turned on the balls of her feet and trotted into the Buy-N-Fly.

Beulah always had to get the last word in.

It was best to keep my mouth shut.

"Hi, Everett." I did feel bad almost hitting him. "How's your momma and them?"

It was always polite manners to ask someone about their family, even if I wasn't listening to the answer.

"Everyone is good." Everett continued to wipe down Beulah's car. I stood there watching because I could feel Beulah Paige inside running her big mouth to everyone in there about me as she paid. "Did you say you saw a cat?"

"Yeah." I pointed to the wooded area next to the Buy-N-Fly. "It must've run off in there."

"I didn't see no cat." His face was clouded with uneasiness.

"Huh." I scratched my head and looked at him. "You didn't?" I asked and watched his head slowly shake back and forth, his eyes never leaving mine.

Suddenly I became increasingly uneasy under his scrutiny.

"Well, it was there." I wasn't waiting for Beulah to come out. I wanted my drink and I wanted it now. With or without Beulah in there gossiping like she always did. Either way, I was going to have to face the music now or later. It would be all over town that I tried to kill her and Everett with my car. Beulah was the gossip queen of Sleepy Hollow and she could pack a tale better than anyone I knew.

"Weee-doggie, I've been dying for a Big Gulp," I proclaimed as loud as I could when I stepped inside the Buy-N-Fly. "Burying dead people all day leaves you a little parched." I slapped my lips open and closed a few times with some sound for dramatic effect.

"See I told ya." Beulah grabbed the pearls around her neck with one hand, guarding them as if I was going to jump her and steal them right off her. "Certifiably nuts."

"You don't know diddly squat," I grumbled under my breath at the Big Gulp counter, filling my cup up to the rim with the pebble ice that made the Diet Coke good and cold. Exactly the way I liked it.

By the time I made it up to the counter to pay, Beulah had hightailed it out of there.

I wish I would've thought to get John Howard Lloyd a drink because when I finally made it to the Sleepy Hollow Cemetery, he was pouring sweat from digging Jade's seven-foot-deep grave plot.

"I wish you would use the backhoe," I said when I approached him.

"Nah." John Howard stopped briefly. He leaned on the shovel with one arm and took his hat off, wiping the sweat away from his wiry hairline with his forearm. "I'm 'bout done. Plus, it keeps me in shape for softball."

"That's right. When is the next game?" I asked about the new softball league that had started back up in Sleepy Hollow.

He shrugged. He was a man of few words.

For years there were teams but it seemed to fade away a while back; but a few months ago John Howard asked me if Eternal Slumber would help sponsor a team and I was game. Especially since Jack Henry was on the team and I loved seeing those tight baseball pants on him.

"Arley Burgin looks like he's practicing sliding on base." I chuckled to myself. John Howard looked confused. "I saw him this morning diving after a bird to put in the fountain in front of Hardgrove's."

He shook his head.

"Are you doing okay?" I asked.

"Sure am, why?"

"I was on my way back to the funeral home and wanted to make sure the final arrangements were all set for Jade's service." I had all the confidence in the world in John Howard. He never failed me.

"You know"—he adjusted his hat before he grabbed the shovel—"I sure am glad you are in charge and Charlotte is gone."

"Is that right?" I asked, fishing for more information.

"Yep." He shook his head. "Arley said your sister is meaner than Gina Marie Hardgrove and he couldn't stand the likes of her." John Howard's mouth thinned in displeasure. "Not that I mean any disrespect to anyone, but I sure wanted you to know how much I'm glad you are here. And business shows it too."

"Not if Beulah has anything to do with it," I muttered, regretting how I had treated her a few minutes ago. At the time it was fun, but Granny would get wind of it from the Auxiliary women and fuss at me like I was ten years old. Marla

Maria all but confirmed they had been gossiping about me when they'd seen me and Granny heading toward Lexington this morning.

"Aw, Miss Bellefry is harmless. She just likes to flap them lips of hers. She ain't got nobody else to listen to her." He winked and stuck the shovel back in the hole, digging a little deeper.

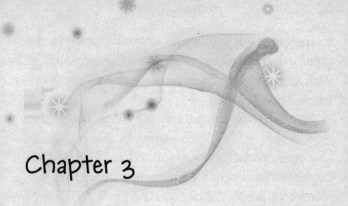

Chapter 3

Everything was looking good at the cemetery and John Howard had it all under control. It was time to make sure Jade was ready to walk her final catwalk in Sleepy Hollow.

Granny's scooter was chained around the tree on the front lawn of the funeral home. I loved Eternal Slumber. It was the prettiest building in Sleepy Hollow, even though I might be a little biased.

The large red brick, two-story home had a beautiful wraparound porch and large concrete steps up the front to the large leaded-glass, wood-framed doors. The wicker furniture on the porch had large comfy pillows that were so inviting. Most visitors in town didn't realize it was a funeral home. They figured it to be a historic home to the area, but my family knew we were in the comforting business and wanted everyone to feel welcome and loved when they came to say good-bye to their loved ones.

"Who in the world put all these flowers in this vestibule?" Granny stood in the middle of the open room when I walked in, surrounded by large floral arrangements. She picked up one that had a big birdhouse attached to it. "This here is from Mable Claire. Now you know she spent all of her social security check on this." Granny tsked.

It was not a secret that the bigger the arrangement sent to a funeral, the better off income-wise the sender was. Everyone tried to outdo everyone. Even with the repass food.

"It was nice of her to send them." I smiled at all the flowers.

"I can't believe the florist would just leave them in here like this." Disappointment sat in Granny's wrinkles. "You better let them know what is what around here because they obviously know you are in charge and they will run over you."

"Dottie and Marla Maria don't really know the protocol, but I'll give her a call and let her know for Sissy's funeral." I picked up an arrangement in each hand and carried them into the viewing room to set them around for the funeral service.

"What do Dottie Kramer and Marla Maria Teater have to do with these?"

"These are straight from Dottie's farm." I was happy to see Jade was laid out and ready to go. I picked up the blue carnation spray Marla had brought over earlier off the front row chairs and carried it over to the casket.

"Are you sure?" Granny asked, following me over to Jade's casket and watching me place the flower spray.

"Yes. Dottie Kramer has opened a flower shop in her barn," I said and adjusted the ribbon to hang a little bit down the front of the casket.

Like always, Granny and I stopped talking, clasped our hands in front of us, bowed our heads and gave a silent prayer for Jade Lee Peel.

"Amen," Granny whispered, lifting her finger, touching each shoulder, her forehead and then her heart.

"Really?" My brows furrowed. "We aren't Catholic," I reminded her.

"I also went back to Hardgrove's to get my papers from Charlotte." I wasn't sure how Granny was going to take it.

I ran my hands over a couple of chair covers on our way out of the viewing room and tugged on the seams to get a few wrinkles out. That was one problem with the blue linens; they showed all the imperfections the dry cleaners couldn't fix and the lint was a problem too.

"Did you get them?" Granny asked.

"I sure did." I pulled the ripped-in-half envelope out of my back pocket and handed it to Granny.

"Oh no." Granny shook her head. "Charlotte Rae is worse off than I thought."

Granny went to the kitchen while I went to my office to change. Artie would be here in no time and I had to be out of my jeans and T-shirt and into my usual undertaking outfit of black pants, black top and a black jacket. There was a note on my desk written by Vernon that my parents had called and to call them ASAP along with the rest of the messages he'd taken earlier.

"Charlotte." I jumped after I turned around and saw her sitting on the couch. "You scared the bejesus out of me. And I've got to go. I don't have time to argue. I'll see you at the service." I stopped shy of the door when I didn't hear her protest. I looked at her. "I told Granny about your behavior," I tattled like a six-year-old little girl. She brought out the worst in me. "The torn-up papers are on my desk. You sign them and I'll tape them back together."

I wasn't about to wait around for her answer or to even respond to me. I scurried down the hall where the vestibule was already buzzing with people coming in to pay their respects.

"Emma, dear," Pastor Brown wrapped his arm in mine when I tried to slip by without being seen. "Artie Peel told me you had a special blue stole for the service. Can I get that?"

"Yes." I snapped my fingers. I had reminded myself earlier not to forget and I wouldn't have if Charlotte hadn't shown up. "Let me grab it out of my office. You stay right here."

Quickly I hurried back down the hall and ducked into the office where I knew Charlotte would be hiding out. She hadn't made an appearance in Sleepy Hollow since she left (except when she'd practically begged Artie to hire her for Jade Lee's funeral). She was afraid everyone was mad at her and image was all she cared about.

"Emma," Charlotte spoke with a low tone. "I'm sorry. I'm really sorry."

"What do you mean?" I shut the door behind me. Charlotte stood next to the window, staring out at the mourning crowd walking up the sidewalk toward the front of Eternal Slumber. "Why are you here? You knew I had a busy day and I don't need you coming in here telling me how wonderful working for Gina Marie is and how much you adore *Sammy Hardgrove*." There was a slight sarcastic tone in my voice.

Charlotte didn't move. Blankly she stared at me.

"Are you okay?" I questioned when I got a good

look at Charlotte Rae. She looked worse now than she did earlier when Granny and I went to see her.

There were a couple of dirt smudges on her light green linen suit around the shoulder area and the neatly tied chocolate scarf was no longer in a loose noose around her neck. It was tighter. I swallowed hard and put my own hands around my neck. It made me cringe.

The knock on the door made me jump.

"Don't tell anyone I'm here," Charlotte said in a tear-smothered voice. A look of half-startled wariness crossed her eyes before she rushed to the office bathroom. "But I do want you to know that I called a carriage company and they will be delivering a Cinderella carriage for Jade to be taken to the cemetery." She walked into the bathroom so as not to be seen.

The office door opened. Granny stood with her hand planted on her hip.

"Who you talking to?" Her eyes darted around the room. "Emma Lee, I asked you a question."

"I . . . um . . ." I gulped and looked toward the bathroom. Charlotte didn't want anyone to know she was there and if I wanted her to sign those papers, I needed to go along with what she wanted. "I was going over my funeral welcome for Jade."

Granny's lips pursed suspiciously. She gave a

slight squint of one eye, a sideways movement of the jaw.

"I know I've done these a million times, but I always like to practice. It's not like Princess Jade will get another funeral and I get a do-over." I smiled, took a deep breath, and rubbed my hands together.

"You are as pretty as a speckled pup." Granny walked over and lifted her hand. She tucked a strand of hair behind my ear. "I know you are upset with Charlotte Rae not signing the papers. You might be a little envious of the big place she's got up there in Lexington. You and I both know she ain't happy up there. So you tuck in whatever is in that pretty little head of yours and go out there and send Jade off in grand style like Artie paid for." She squeezed. "Nice touch with that Cinderella carriage."

Granny jerked me toward her and gave me a big bear hug. Over her shoulder, the bathroom door quietly opened. Charlotte Rae stuck her head out. Her eyes seared into me. Slowly she shook her head and lifted her finger to her lips. A slight "shh" escaped her mouth and she shut the door.

"Now." Granny pushed me out to arm's length. "I'm going out to greet some folks. Put a little lipstick on and get out there." Granny didn't wait for me to say anything. She wasn't going to hear of it. She and I both knew I had a job to do.

I couldn't help but laugh. Granny thought lipstick solved everything.

"We did go see Charlotte." Granny stood in the middle of Beulah, Mable, Hettie, Marla and Mary Anna. "You wouldn't believe all the responsibility she has on her shoulders."

I watched as all the Auxiliary women leaned as Granny wove a tale of Charlotte to put to rest any gossip the women might've started. As much as I wanted to march over there and tell them the truth, I restrained myself.

"She is so good at making everyone happy. She hosts weddings and funerals." I overheard Granny bragging on when I walked past and straightened the memorial cards that were placed on a stand stationed before you walked into the viewing room.

The people paying respect for Jade had died down and people were beginning to take their seats. Pastor Brown stood up in front by the casket and placed his Bible on the podium. His razor-sharp blue eyes looked at me and he gave a little nod, letting me know he was ready. He ran his hand over his slick black hair. The sleeve on his brown pin-striped suit coat was a little too small, hitting above his wrist bone, exposing a tarnished metal watch. He cleared his throat.

I turned and walked around, whispering to the small gathered groups that we were ready to start. Everyone walked into the viewing room and took an empty seat. John Howard stood in the hallway and flipped on the sound system. "Blessed Assurance" crackled through the old speakers.

A cackle from the vestibule caught my attention as Granny walked over to me to stand in the back.

"What is Charlotte doing?" I groaned and gave my sister the stink eye when I realized it was her laughing. She took a seat next to the sideboard table. "She told me she didn't want anyone to know she was here. And now she's making fun of the sound system."

"Hi-do." Granny nodded at a couple of late folks as they walked by and took a seat in the back of the viewing room. "Where is she?"

"By the sideboard," I bent over and whispered. Charlotte smiled her pretty smile, crossed her long, lean legs and twiddled her fingers in the air at me, giving me a little wink. A wink in Sleepy Hollow said more than a thousand words. "Uh." I glared at her. "Of course she didn't mean it. She wants everyone to see her," I whispered.

"Where?" Granny asked again. Her eyes darted around the vestibule.

"In the chair." I pointed to Charlotte in the chair. "Oh." My mind reeled. "If she thinks she's going to sit there by that sideboard after I told her that she couldn't have it, she's got another thing coming to her." I wagged my finger at Charlotte.

Granny smacked my hand.

"Emma Lee Raines, that chair is empty." Granny put her hand up on my forehead. "Are you getting sick? Have you taken your meds?"

"So you really can see dead people?" Charlotte Rae was suddenly next to me. "And you really don't have the 'Funeral Trauma'?"

Suddenly things had become very clear.

Charlotte Rae Raines wasn't there to visit her family home, make amends with me, sign the papers or help me with Jade Lee Peel's funeral. She was there as a Betweener client.

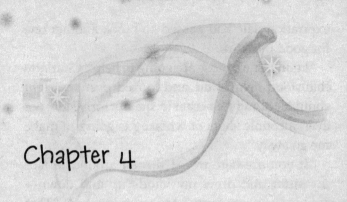

Chapter 4

"This is not happening." I tried to swallow the lump in my throat and hurried back to the bathroom in my office. It was the only place for privacy, especially during a funeral.

I'd left Granny to tend to latecomers. All she had to do was stand in the back as Pastor Brown said his eulogy.

I locked the bathroom door behind me and opened the medicine cabinet door above the sink.

"Where are you?" I fingered the pill bottles on the shelves until I came across the medication Doc Clyde had prescribed for me for the "Funeral Trauma." I unscrewed the lid and popped one in my mouth. I looked at the bottle and noticed the expiration date had passed so I took another one for good measure.

"I don't think those are going to help." Charlotte Rae stood behind me and looked over my right shoulder at my reflection in the mirror. "Hell, not even a couple shots of whiskey is going to make me go away."

"If you are here in"—I turned around to face my sister and drew my hands up and down—"in . . . in ghost form." My voice cracked. "That means that you were . . ." I swallowed. Hard. "Murdered."

"I think I put up a fight." She ran her hands down her green skirt, trying to brush the dirt off. She fussed with her messy hair. "Honestly, do you think that I'd look like this if I didn't?"

A tear trickled down my face. My heart was breaking in half. Charlotte Rae and I might've had our differences, but I never wished her dead. Or worse. Murdered.

"Emma Lee Raines, you get yourself together right this minute." Charlotte Rae fussed. "You are tougher than a pine knot. And I don't want to see you grieving over me while I'm here. I want you to get of your keister, and find out who killed me and why."

I opened my mouth. No words came out. My

chest felt like it had a twenty-pound weight on it as I tried to take a breath. My body shivered. My hands felt cold as though all the blood had drained from my extremities.

"Okay." Charlotte smiled. "Why don't you tell me about this gift you have?"

"Well." I looked at my sister. Every bit of resentment I had for her had silently drifted away as if it'd never happened. "Do you remember when that snowman from Artie's fell on me when I went down there to get us lunch?"

She nodded.

"When I woke up, you and Granny were on one side of my hospital bed." I bit back more tears. "On the other was Chicken Teater and Ruthie Sue Payne. They were so excited that I could see them. I swear I thought I was—" I stopped myself.

"Dead? Like me?" Charlotte took the words out of my mouth.

I nodded. "Jack Henry and I went to see a psychic and she told me that I was given the gift of a Betweener. I help people who have been murdered figure out who killed them so they can cross over."

"Oh." Charlotte Rae's mouth formed an O. "Well." She shook her head, flinging her red curls behind her shoulders. She straightened her shoulders and looked at me. "Ahem," she cleared her throat as though she too were holding back the tears. "I reckon you need to stop feeling sorry for yourself and get to figuring out who killed me."

"And just how do you think I can do that?" I stomped. "You are my sister. The others were just people in the community. But this." I lifted my hands in the air and tilted my chin to the sky as if the Big Guy was listening. "How do you expect me to get through this one?"

"Just like you did the others," Charlotte Rae answered.

"Where is your body?" I asked.

She shrugged. "The last thing I remember was working at the funeral home. Someone had come up behind me and I clawed at them."

"In the funeral home?" I asked and pointed to her dirty skirt. "Where did the dirt come from?"

Her normally pretty face contorted. She looked down.

"So we know that you weren't killed in your office." It only made sense since she was dirty and Charlotte never liked to get dirty, so by reasoning, I knew she hadn't willingly gotten dirty.

"Good question." Her voice was flat. Her green eyes narrowed speculatively.

"What?" I asked, curious to what was going on in her ghost mind.

"I was just thinking this whole sleuthing thing just might be fun." She rubbed her hands together.

"It's not as great as it sounds." I eyed her. "Do you even know the scope of you being my client?"

Her face set, her jaw clenched, and her eyes fixed on me.

"I have to tell Mom and Dad and Granny that you're dead," I said in a shaky voice. "I have to put my grief aside and help find your killer."

"Now you decide to get selfish?" Charlotte laughed. "You're not the selfish one. I am." She pointed to herself.

"Selfish?" I drew back. "You are dead. My only sister. My only sibling."

There was a knock on the door.

"Geez." Charlotte twirled on her heels. "Don't they know you are in the bathroom?"

"Emma." Jack Henry Ross called my name. "Honey, I need to talk to you. Zula Fae said that you were upset and said something about seeing Charlotte. I'm worried about you."

There was no sense in keeping it from Jack. He'd know soon enough when the Lexington authorities came to tell us that Charlotte Rae Raines was a victim of homicide.

"Come on in." I took a quick look out the door before I closed it behind him. Everything looked fine at Jade's funeral and I was sure Granny was being a great hostess.

I planted myself up against the back of the door and looked at Jack.

"I guess you should know that I am seeing Charlotte. She's sitting right over there." I pointed to the couch. Jack Henry looked in the empty space and then slid his eyes to me.

"You mean?" Jack made a slight gesture with his hand referring to a Betweener client like he'd always done.

I stared blankly at him with my mouth open. I could feel my nostrils flare as I tried to hold back tears. I nodded.

A stab of guilt lay buried in my breast. I had been so mean to Charlotte; it didn't matter how she had treated me. It was the last real interaction I had had with her human self.

"Oh, Emma." Jack Henry drew me in his arms. He used the heel of his shoe to shut the door behind him, drowning out the crowd of mourners there for Jade Lee. He ran his strong hand down my head, petting me like a puppy. "I'm so sorry," he whispered and snugged me tighter.

We stayed there for a few minutes.

"Ahem," Charlotte cleared her throat. "I'm y'all's number one fan and all, but can we get on with this?"

"Yes." I stepped back and wiped the tears from my face.

"Yes what?" Jack Henry looked at me with the sympathetic eyes I knew all too well. They were the same eyes that I gave to the families of my Eternal Slumber clients.

"Charlotte." I couldn't cry for laughing. "She's telling us to get on with it."

"I understand that this"—he gestured between me and him—"is separate than this." He pointed to the door at the funeral home. "I still have to tell your granny. Your parents."

"My granny." A glazed look of despair crossed my face. "My parents."

There was nothing worse than telling a deceased family member of the demise of the loved one. Especially the passing of a child. Not that Charlotte was a little child, but she was still my parents' child. There was nothing good that was going to come from this.

"Can we wait until after Jade's funeral service?" I asked. Not that any time was going to be better. "Or at least until the Lexington authorities confirm it. I just don't think it would be good to dump on them that Charlotte is dead before she's reported dead."

Jack looked at me. His eyes searched my face as

though he was trying to read my feelings. "Yeah. I guess you're right."

I was numb. I was sick to my stomach. This was going way beyond my Betweener duties and I wasn't sure if I was going to be able to keep it together. Before it was all said and done, the fine citizens of Sleepy Hollow just might see me with a real case of the "Funeral Trauma."

Chapter 5

It was not easy, but somehow I did pull it together for Jade Lee Peel's repass, which was the supper after the funeral. The Auxiliary women hosted it in the basement of the Sleepy Hollow Baptist Church and it meant that as soon as the carriage dropped Jade's casket off at the cemetery, my job was done.

Generally my mouth watered thinking about the food served at the repass, but not today. Today I was probably going to skip out early and make an excuse that I had to get Sissy ready for her big day in the morning.

But still, I was going to miss the food that was exquisitely prepared by the Auxiliary. The local high school football rivalries were kitten fights compared to the competition between the women in the Auxiliary, including Granny. They always brought their A game in the food department. One trying to outdo the other. Everyone kept score on who complimented their food, and at the end of the night, the Auxiliary women compared notes and someone always came out on top, upping the game for the next repass, which in this case would be Sissy Phillips's.

Granny had a cherry pie to die for and Beulah Paige had a chicken pot pie that was gobbled up on the first pass of the food line. Of course it was always fun and exciting to watch when one of the Auxiliary women brought something that wasn't on the list. Oh yeah. There was a list that was kept and checked off when you dropped off your dish. The keeper of the list happened to be Granny.

"Did you get a piece of Zula Fae's pie?" I heard someone say when I passed by one of the banquet tables. "Delish."

I looked at Granny, who was standing behind the open window where you could see the women working away in the kitchen and gave her a thumbs-up.

She licked her pointer finger and gave herself an imaginary mark in the win column. I gave her a quick wave and mouthed that I had to go back and work on Sissy. She gave me the a-okay sign.

The sun was shining and the birds were chirping on my hop and skip back down the town square toward Eternal Slumber. I wanted to enjoy the lovely walk, but I knew I had limited time alone. Vernon, John Howard and Mary Anna were still filling their bellies in the basement of the church but I had enough time to get back to the funeral home and find out more about Charlotte.

I ran up the front steps and opened the big doors. Charlotte was still sitting in the chair next to the sideboard. She looked up, a wry grin on her face as she wiped slow rubs on top of the antique piece of furniture.

"I'll be." She brought her hands up and smacked them together in delight. "After all this time you really were telling the truth. You *can* see dead people. I mean I thought you were nuts. Coo-coo crazy like everyone else in Sleepy Hollow thought, but you aren't. I mean you can see dead people."

Charlotte went on and on. I fell back into the couch with my eyes closed tight and praying on exactly how I was going to solve my sister's murder while I grieved, and was there for my family.

"Were you really getting Mamie Sue's teeth for her that night you broke into Burns Funeral Home and got caught?"

"Yes." I couldn't help but smile thinking how my Betweener client, Mamie Sue Preston, was buried without her dentures and I had to break into Burns Funeral Home to get them out of her file so I could slip them into her grave.

I might be good at helping ghosts cross over, but I was not good at breaking the law. It embarrassed Jack Henry to death when I got caught and I'm not even going to try to recall how Granny nearly died right in the kitchen of the inn when one of the gossipy Auxiliary women told Granny I had broken into our number one competitor.

Jack knew my secret about seeing the dead so I got a little sympathy from him. Not much. But a little.

"And the time you joined the beauty pageant." Charlotte flopped down next to me. "Were you doing that to help Chicken Teater cross over?"

"Yes." I laughed thinking about how I had let Mary Anna turn me into a blonde for the sake of helping these ghosts. Trust me, blondes don't have more fun.

"I'll be." Charlotte grinned from ear to ear. "You can see ghosts."

"I'm a Betweener." It was like a big weight had been lifted off my shoulders as I sat there and told Charlotte everything that I had been keeping from everyone.

Suddenly it hit me. My hands started to shake. "Oh, Charlotte." I burst into tears. The realization that *my sister* was a ghost suddenly hit me hard. "Who? When? I was just with you. Granny. Momma. Daddy." I couldn't bring myself to even say the words that would devastate my family.

"I don't know what happened. One minute I was at Hardgrove's in my office, the next minute I'm here." She looked down at her suit and tried to brush off the dirt. "This suit was expensive too."

The cat I'd been trying to catch ran over, jumping into Charlotte's lap.

"I'm not its ghost. He's lost." Charlotte rubbed down the cat's fur.

"What?" My eyes shot open. "It's a ghost cat?"

"You can see animals too?" Charlotte asked a good question.

The orange tabby purred with each swipe of Charlotte's hands. Its back arched when her long nails raked down its spine.

"Apparently," I groaned flatly wondering why on earth it was here.

"I never knew you liked cats." It was weird seeing Charlotte give anything any of her time when she was mostly conceited and selfish.

"I never said I didn't like cats. I just don't think someone should have a pet if they don't have time to take care of the pet." She smiled, blinking slowly at the cat. "I heard on the Animal Network that cats like to be blinked at slowly."

"Ghost Charlotte is much nicer than living Charlotte." I shrugged.

"Gee thanks," she grumbled.

The cat curled up on her lap with its paws tucked up under its chin. This was a first for me as a Betweener. All of my Betweener clients had been people I'd had as clients at Eternal Slumber or who were residents of Sleepy Hollow.

My brows creased and I chewed on the inside of my cheek as I thought about the ghost cat. It was going to have to wait until I figured out Charlotte Rae's situation. I was going to have to get used to having a pet until then. Not to mention that I needed to go back to see the psychic Jack Henry had taken me to when we first needed confirmation and clarification I had this so-called gift. It was my understanding that I was only seeing the ghosts of murdered Eternal Slumber clients. Then I had ghosts that were just community members. And now the cat. I had a sneaky suspicion the psychic was going to have more eye-opening news about my gift than I wanted to hear.

I looked over at Charlotte Rae. She was so content sitting there with that cat that it sort of made me uneasy. She'd never been one to just sit and do nothing.

"But if I help you cross over"—I bit back the tears—"it means I'll never see you again."

"Oh, you'll see me again. In the ever after." She reached over and patted me. "You have to help me. I can't stay here in this between stage forever. It's not good for my complexion."

Charlotte was wrong. It wasn't fair that she looked just as pretty as a ghost as she did as a living person. When I first saw her as a ghost, she looked a little tired, but hope filled her green eyes, bringing the sparkle back.

"But I can't let you go." The tears streamed down my face. "I know we have had our differences, but . . ."

She stopped me by putting her finger on my mouth.

"Shh." Charlotte smiled. "I know you love me. You don't have to keep telling me about our differences. We are different. Everyone is different. But we are blood. You will always be my sister and that is what's important."

"Why didn't you sign the papers?" I asked. I guess it didn't matter now that she was dead that she didn't sign them, but I needed to know for my peace of mind.

"I don't know." She placed a flat palm on her stomach. "A gut feeling."

"I haven't failed yet." I took a deep breath.

"You mean you have helped more than Ruthie and Chicken?" Charlotte's green eyes opened wide.

Slowly I nodded. "Cephus, Digger, Mamie and Jade Lee too."

Charlotte's jaw dropped wide open. Rarely was Charlotte left speechless.

I laughed, hoping to break the tension between us.

"I can't believe I treated you like you were crazy." She smacked the palm of her hand to her forehead. "I made you take those 'Funeral Trauma' pills Doc Clyde gave you."

"I pretended to take them," I assured her. I did take a few, but all of that didn't seem relevant now. "Seeing the ghosts did make me feel crazy at first, but now it's strange if I'm not surrounded by them. Just like you keep telling me to forget about our differences, stop apologizing for thinking I was crazy." I held up my thumb and forefinger and parted them a fraction. "I might be a tad bit nuts." I winked.

"Do you see anyone else? Like now?" Her head twisted as she looked around the room.

"Nope. Just you." I paused and looked at the feline. "And that cat."

I had seen two ghosts at once before when the murderer was the same, but I hoped Charlotte

Rae's situation wasn't the same. Two ghosts at once was almost too much. Even ghosts bicker back and forth like children. Fighting over who gets more of your time.

"I have no idea about the cat. I can only tell you that it's not with me." Charlotte did a little shimmy shake.

There was a light rap on the door.

"Emma Lee." Charlotte stopped me when I got up to answer the door. I had to face the music at some point. "What is next?"

"Well." I turned toward her. "We wait for someone to call us about your fate. It's not like I can go run and inform people that you are dead when no one has found your body. Then I look for clues about who did it and Jack Henry puts the son-ofabitch behind bars. I would like to kill whoever did this, but I don't want them to haunt me." My lips formed a thin line across my face. I tried to tip up the edges, but they fell into a frown. My eyes teared up again. "I'm not sure what I'm going to do without you."

"You'll be just fine." Charlotte disappeared into thin air just as the knock at the door got louder.

"Emma Lee?" Jack Henry's voice was on the other side.

I opened the door to find Jack Henry and Granny standing behind him with curious eyes staring back at me. I was sure Jack had held Granny off as long as he could, giving me a little time alone with Charlotte.

"I'm so sorry." I ran my hands down my suit jacket. "My blood sugar must be low. I've been so worked up about Charlotte not signing the papers." The excuse was lame, but the last thing I wanted to tell Granny was that she was about to get a call to let her know Charlotte Rae was dead.

"Enough about the stupid papers!" Charlotte chirped from the other room.

"Not that the papers matter." I shook my head and smiled at Granny.

"Are you sure you're okay?" Granny slightly pushed Jack Henry to the side. I used *slightly* very generously. "I know you didn't just say those papers didn't matter. What Charlotte Rae did to you was a humdinger of a doozy."

"You've got to be kidding me." Charlotte's ghost was suddenly standing next to me. "Granny is on your side?"

"Plus that sideboard." Granny tapped her finger to her forehead before she circled one of her red curls around it. "I've been thinking on that. At first when she asked for it, I didn't give two hoots and a holler, but you're right."

"Right?" Charlotte stomped. Good ole Charlotte was coming back. "Don't you get me started, old lady." Charlotte's eyes narrowed as she warned Granny.

I giggled. I just couldn't help it. Ghost Charlotte was pitchin' a fit right there in front of Granny as Granny talked about her. I giggled again, trying to stop by placing my hand over my mouth.

Jack Henry was a nervous Nellie, fidgeting side to side, not knowing what to do. I could tell he didn't know whether to take Granny's side or try to understand my giggling, though I could tell he knew it was all Charlotte's doing.

"Boy, you got ants in your pants?" Granny's eyes did a long slow slide toward Jack. "What's wrong with you?"

"Nothing, ma'am." Jack's lips pressed together. He knew all too well the wrath of Zula Fae Raines Payne. Lord have mercy on whoever did this to Charlotte Rae, because they would have to face Granny.

Chapter 6

No matter how much I tried and how much Charlotte Rae encouraged me, I just didn't get one ounce of sleep. Jack Henry had been busy on the computer with his police websites looking up crimes in the area to see if anything about Charlotte had come through. Nothing had shown up which made me believe that no one had found her yet, and that just broke my heart.

It's not good to be dead, but to be dead when no one has found your body was just plumb awful. No amount of time alone with Jack Henry or Preparation H was going to help my stress go away. But a big cup of coffee from Higher Grounds Café would help jump-start my day.

"Hey, Sug." Mary Anna Hardy was sitting at a

four-top table with Beulah Paige, Bea Allen and
Mable Claire at Higher Grounds Café sipping
their coffees and eating their fresh baked soufflés.
"Are you all right? You look tired."

"Thanks for the compliment." I shook my head.
If Charlotte's body had been found, this would've
been an altogether different conversation.

"Or are you just so worried about Sissy's funeral this morning?" Bea Allen's lips curled up
in a snarky grin. Her frizzy hair topped the six-
foot body that was slumped back in the chair. She
swung her leg that was crossed over the other to
and fro, letting that big toe of hers stick out like a
sore thumb. It wasn't her prettiest quality.

"Really, you need to tell her that she needs to
wear closed-toe shoes." Charlotte's nose curled in
a phew-wee curl.

I swallowed, trying to stay focused on the
women.

"Why would I be worried about Sissy's funeral?" I asked, wondering what she meant.

She shrugged her shoulders, a smug look on her
face.

"I think Emma Lee has been doing a good job."
Mable Claire's cheeks balled up from her big grin.
She snapped her fingers as a child walked by, stopping the little boy. "Here, honey." She dug deep in
her pocket and took out a penny. She held it up

to her eyes before sticking it back in her pocket. The little boy snarled. "You are a big boy. A penny won't even let you buy a piece of candy over at Artie's." She dug deeper in her pocket and took out a nickel. Proud, she held it out to him. "Here you go. Don't go spending all that in one place."

The little boy looked at the coin and smiled politely, stepping out of the way before more children with doughnuts in one hand held out the other hand as Mable Claire gave each one a coin. This was her. She clinked when she walked from all the change, and every child she passed got a coin.

"Thank you, Mable Claire." I took a little bow from behind the line of children, and then turned toward Beulah Paige Bellefry. "Beulah?"

"Tell Beulah to stop going to the tanning bed." Charlotte's ghost had all of a sudden gotten a backbone. Never in a million years would living Charlotte ever say these things about these women. "And those lashes. I wonder how much she paid for those."

Charlotte was right. Everything on Beulah Paige was fake. Even her eyelashes. Recently I'd heard that she'd even gotten her eyebrows threaded. Whatever that was. It just meant another thing on her was not real. Just like the smile on her face wasn't real.

"Going for a new look?" I questioned Beulah's long red hair that had a more toned-down look.

"Yeah." Mary Anna leaned back and crossed her arms in front of her. "I've been meaning to ask you about that." She glared at Beulah. Beulah shifted in her seat and fiddled with the edges of her napkin.

"And your brows look different." I bent down. Beulah glared at me.

Mary Anna jumped up, knocking down the chair behind her. The entire café went silent and all eyes were on us. "You have been going to someone different." Mary Anna knew that the new color wasn't done by her hands, nor were the brows. "You've been cheating on me." The hurt dripped out of her mouth.

"I was trying something different. But I don't like it." Beulah ran her fingers through her hair and threw it behind her shoulders. "I'll be at Girl's Best Friend to get it fixed."

"It's gonna cost ya." Mary Anna shook her finger before she stomped out of the café door.

"You are always causing problems," Bea Allen grunted from her seat.

"From what I hear, Burns has been making a lot of mistakes." It might not have been a nice thing to say, but it was a thing between me and my biggest competitor.

"Where on earth did you hear that?" Bea jerked back. "You heard wrong. We are plenty busy. Right, Beulah?"

"Right as rain." Beulah nodded.

"Here's your coffee," Cheryl Lynne Doyle called from behind the counter to me. It was my cue to leave or that Cheryl wanted me to stop teasing her customers.

When I walked off, I heard Beulah say, "My hair looks good, doesn't it?"

"Don't you pay no attention to that Emma Lee," Bea assured her.

I couldn't help but smile. Usually they were the ones getting my goat and today I got theirs.

"They are just mean," Charlotte grumbled and pressed her nose up against the glass counter like a child. "If I'd known I was going to die so young, I'd gotten me a few of these instead of trying to watch my figure all the time."

"You know—" I took what Charlotte said to heart. We never knew when it was our time to go. I surely wouldn't have thought it was Charlotte's. "I'll take a caramel long john to go."

"Wow," Cheryl Lynne, my longtime high school classmate and friend, had surprise in her voice. "Look at you." She stepped back and put her hands on her lean hips.

Cheryl was born with a silver spoon in her

mouth. She'd gone to New York City and seen those fancy coffee cafés. She told her daddy she wanted one so she went to barista school while her daddy bought and fixed up the building that was now Higher Grounds Café.

She did good business and she was good with customers. We'd actually become close friends.

"Life is too short not to enjoy a long john every once in a while." I peeled a couple dollars out of my front jeans pocket and laid them on the counter.

"I like your thinking." She handed me a bag with the Higher Grounds logo and my large coffee. "I've got some bagels and dip to drop by Eternal Slumber for Sissy's repass this morning. I figured bagels were a good brunch food. Where you off to?"

"Fiddling. Finishing touches," I lied.

I couldn't wait any longer. I had to drive to Lexington and go to Hardgrove's. I had to find Charlotte's body. It was killing me keeping this from Granny and my parents.

My phone chirped from my pocket. It was Jack Henry. I let it go to voice mail.

"If I'm not at Eternal Slumber when you drop off the bagels, just stick them in the fridge." It wasn't like I needed to be there. The funeral home was always unlocked during the day. After all, it was a business.

The one good thing when Charlotte was there was that she was there all the time. With only me, it was hard to be there and do all the other things that needed to be done for funerals. Now I had this ghost issue on my plate, which was of the utmost importance to me right now.

I took some time eating my doughnut while driving out of town toward Hardgrove's. I wanted a little distance between me and Sleepy Hollow before I called Jack Henry back because if he knew where I was going, he'd try to stop me.

"What's going on?" I asked Jack when he answered.

"Nothing," Jack Henry said in a flat voice. "Are you sure that you are seeing her?"

"Really?" I asked. "You're questioning me?"

"It just seems weird that no one has reported her missing from work." Jack had a good point but it was exactly why I was going to Hardgrove's.

"Glad you brought that up. I'm on my way to Hardgrove's as we speak." The hearse hugged the curves of the back roads between Sleepy Hollow and Lexington.

"Turn around right now," Jack ordered me. "If there is something going on, let the police handle it."

"No." The nerve of him. "There was something that went on and Charlotte is right here.

I'm going to find her body and get this investigation done."

It occurred to me that I had no idea how Charlotte had died. Everything I uncovered was going to be out of pure luck. The only place I knew to start was her office where I'd last left her and her words, *One minute I was at Hardgrove's with you and now I'm here.*

If Hardgrove's was the last place she remembered being, then that was my starting point.

"I even had a buddy from the Lexington force head over to Charlotte's apartment and he said there was no one home. Her car wasn't in the parking lot either." Jack was good about doing his due diligence.

My only problem was he knew she wasn't going to answer the door.

"Of course she didn't answer. She's dead!" Frustrated, I yelled into the phone. "You know what." I let out a deep sigh. "I've got to go."

"Emma, don't get mad." Jack's voice softened. "I know this situation is a little too close to home."

"Too close?" I asked. "It is close. It is home. You can't get much closer than your own flesh and blood. Oh, but you don't have a sibling," I growled. "You only have your mommy and daddy," I said in a baby voice.

His mommy and daddy were a hot button

topic with us. At least that was what I called them because they still treated him like he was two years old.

Or I might've been a little sensitive because his mother did everything in her power to keep us apart. Even turned in his application to the Kentucky State Police Department, where he would have had to move away from Sleepy Hollow and from me. Her plan.

"Don't go bringing my parents into this," he warned. "You know they like you."

Jack had always wanted to work his way up into the ranks of the state police and beyond. It was true that Jack didn't apply because he knew he'd have to move away from me and there was no way in hell I was moving away from Sleepy Hollow.

Some folks I grew up with couldn't wait to get out of our little town, while I just sat back and enjoyed the slow-paced life. Since I'd become a Betweener life had picked up a bit.

"Emma, you are stressed. The best thing for you to do is to go back to Eternal Slumber and make sure Sissy's funeral is ready. Let me get my buddy to go to Hardgrove's and check it out." Jack was always the voice of reason, but I didn't want to hear reason.

I was hankering for an argument. I was mad.

Real mad. Angry, in fact. And I had to take it out on someone.

"Did you tell your buddy that I'm crazy and see dead people?" My gift had become my curse and was proving that my high school nickname might just be true. Creepy Funeral Girl.

"Don't be ridiculous." Jack Henry sounded fed up. He sighed deeply into the phone. "I'm not going to pick a fight with you. You are overly sensitive for good reason. All I'm asking is that you turn around and let my buddy from the Lexington PD go over there and see what he finds."

"Okay." I crossed my fingers and held on to the wheel, pushing the pedal to the floor even more.

"Okay?" Jack asked with a surprised tone. "Good. I'll see you at Sissy's funeral unless my buddy digs up something." He let a moment of silence pass before he said, "I love you, Emma Lee."

"Love you too." I threw the phone in the seat between me and Charlotte Rae.

When I said "love you too," he knew that was me saying it because I was mad. When I said "I love you," he knew I meant it from the bottom of my heart. No matter how much he made sense, there was no way I was going to turn around when I was almost there.

"That didn't sound so good." Charlotte

drummed her long fingernails on the passenger door.

"Here is the thing with me and Jack Henry." It was kind of nice being able to have girl talk with my sister about my relationship with Jack. Before she never had time to listen and didn't want to. "We are great as boyfriend and girlfriend. He has the best manners in the world."

"I feel a but." Charlotte beat me to the next part of the story.

"But . . ." I took a deep breath and turned into Hardgrove's driveway. The big fountain spouted water and the swans were happily swimming around and around. "I'm a Betweener and he is a cop, so it clashes. He likes how I can give him the clues he needs to solve the murders, only he wants me to stay away from following the clues."

"Oh." Charlotte's brows lifted. She stopped drumming her fingernails and crossed her arms across her chest.

"Yeah." Not the reassuring advice I wanted my big sister to give me, but Granny didn't perfect her sweet tea in a day. "Of course I can't do that. When I have a Betweener client who has a clue or I stumble upon one, I'm going to investigate to see the validity of the clue before I hand it over to him."

"Like me," Charlotte said with a helpless wave of her hand.

For a split second, I'd forgotten Charlotte was a client, making my heart drop again.

"The issue with you is that I don't know where your physical body is located." The thought of my sister's lifeless body somewhere put a knot in my throat. I swallowed, hard. "I want to find you. Put finding the killer aside. I want to find my sister."

"He thinks it's part of the crime." She looked out the window at the Legacy Center. Her car was still there parked in the parking space that had a metal sign cemented in the driveway with her name printed on it. "Because I'm sure he's right."

"Of course you would take up for him." I rolled my eyes.

"No, I've watched a lot of crime TV shows and where there is a body, there is usually evidence," she boasted with pride in her voice.

This was when ghost Charlotte sounded exactly like mortal Charlotte.

I turned in my seat and looked at her. I said in a matter-of-fact kind of way, "You are my sister." I turned back around with my keys and phone in my hand ready to get out. "Oh my God!" I screamed and planted my hand on my heart when I noticed Arley Burgin's face planted on my driver's side window.

"Golly. You all right, Miss Emma?" he asked when he opened my door. Even though he had a crooked smile, his gray eyes drooped underneath his shaggy blond hair. He scratched his wispy goatee. "What you doing here?"

"I stopped by to see my sister." I smiled and locked the hearse door behind me. "I heard you don't think too much of her."

"That big-mouth John Howard." Arley had an aw-shucks look on his face. In a swift move, he scuffed the bottom of his shoe on the pavement. "I guess you gonna tell her."

Charlotte Rae stomped over in her fancy high-heeled shoes. She jabbed her fists on her thin hips and leaned into Arley's face.

"I gave you a job, you ungrateful little . . ." At that moment, Charlotte reminded me of one of those cartoon characters we used to watch when we were kids on Saturday morning when they had fumes coming out of their ears, only Charlotte was much prettier.

"Of course I won't tell her." I smiled.

"He's so ungrateful." Charlotte's perfectly pouty lips thinned in anger. She stuck her finger in his face. "Are you the sonofabitch that killed me?"

I laughed.

"Are you sure you're all right?" he asked.

"Oh, I'm fine." It was funny how Charlotte assumed Arley was a suspect. Rookie. "I'll see you later."

"Okay, Miss Emma." He moved out of the way and I stepped around him. "Miss Emma?" He stopped me. "Are you still okay with me being on the Eternal Slumber softball team?"

"Heck yeah." I smiled.

"Thanks." He took the hat off his head and held it to his chest. "You never know when someone finds out that their people have been talked about. I sure didn't mean for it to get back to ya."

By people, I knew he meant family.

"Don't worry about it." I waved it off and headed on into Hardgrove's. It wasn't like what he said wasn't true. I knew firsthand that she was a pill to work with.

The glass doors slid open and the receptionist was sitting behind the desk, talking into her headset. She didn't have the old push-button desk phone I had. She held up a hand when I tried to walk back to Charlotte's office.

I waited patiently until she took down some information for yet another wedding client.

"Can I help you?" She curled her hand over her microphone in front of her mouth. Her brows rose.

"I'm here to see my sister." I gestured down the hall toward Charlotte's office.

"I'm sorry, she's gone on vacation. You'll have

to come back when she gets here." The woman hit another button and answered the other line.

"Hell, I hope I went somewhere warm and sunny." Charlotte Rae cackled. She leaned on her elbow up against the receptionist's desk and drummed her long fingernails on top.

"That's weird," I interrupted the woman. My head tilted to the side, my brows furrowed. A little sarcastic tone came out of my mouth. "She never said anything to me and Granny about going on vacation." I straightened up and shrugged. "I just need to get my paperwork I left for her."

I began to walk past the receptionist's desk.

"Oh," Charlotte tsked. "She's not going to like that," Charlotte warned.

"Whoa! Whoa!" The word came out very loud and very clear. "I said whoa! Whoa!"

I picked up the pace when I heard the wheels on her rolling desk chair squeak. She was coming for me. Picking up the pace, I took off in a dead sprint down the hall until I slipped into Charlotte's office and locked the door behind me.

"Whoa! Whoa!" The girl beat on the door. Suddenly Yosemite Sam from the childhood cartoon popped in my head. The one where he was riding that camel, bouncing up and down and yelling whoa until the camel finally threw him off and Yosemite Sam cracked the animal on the head with his shotgun. Thank God the woman didn't have a shotgun.

"Oh my God!" There was pleasure in Charlotte's voice from the other side of the door. "She's using her flat palm to bang on the door."

"You better open the door or I'm calling the police!" The woman shrieked; the banging was becoming faster and louder.

"She will." Charlotte ghosted herself next to the desk where I was rummaging around the top of it.

"So." I didn't pay the woman's threat much attention.

"So?" Charlotte questioned. "But you will go to jail."

Phew. I rolled my eyes. "This is part of the Betweener gig." I shuffled the files around her desk trying to see if anything popped out at me. Charlotte's calendar was sitting on top. I scanned down it to see who she had appointments with. "I have to get in here and see if there are any clues."

"I'm here. I'm dead. What other clues do you need?" she asked sharply.

"Oh, I don't know, maybe clues about who killed you." I looked up and took my phone out of my back pocket.

"Oh." She had a perplexed look on her face. "Now what are you doing?"

"I'm taking a photo of your calendar so I can

visit these people." I clicked away, turning the pages. There was no time to analyze the appointments because the distant sound of sirens echoed. That damn receptionist kept her word. "Where are your files?"

"In there." She pointed to a credenza on the other side of her office.

I hurried over, trying to beat the sirens coming closer and closer. With my phone in my hand, I used my thumb to go down the photos of her calendar while my other hand pulled out the client files. My ears perked when I heard a car door slam outside. I stood up; my eyes darted back and forth between the door and the window.

"I told her not to go in there!" The woman's shrill voice was faint from the other side of the office door.

I grabbed the files and hurried over to the window. I set the files on the windowsill and looked out. Charlotte's office was facing the fountain. I opened the window and looked down. There were bushes under her window, so I threw the files out next to them.

The hearse was parked pretty close to Charlotte's window and I looked to judge the distance, wondering if I could just jump out the window, grab the files and run to the hearse.

"Are you sure you're okay?" Arley appeared

next to the bushes. He had a metal rake in his hands. His eyes drew down to the files scattered on the ground around his feet.

"Arley." I was never so glad to see him. "I need you to grab those files and stick them under my car tires."

His eyes lowered and he paused a second.

"Open up!" The police officer's voice boomed behind the locked door in a demanding voice.

"Please." I wasn't beyond begging or bribing. "I'll buy all new equipment for the softball team this year."

Arley dropped the rake and gathered the files. I didn't wait by the window to see if he did what I asked. I just put the window down and went to the door.

"Can I help you?" I asked and ducked as a police baton swung a little too close to my head.

"Sorry." The young officer's face popped open in surprise as he put the baton back on his belt. "I was going to knock again."

"That's her! Arrest her for trespassing!" The receptionist pouted and stomped.

"Ma'am, I understand that you are not an employee here and not"—he paused, looked past me and read the nameplate on the door—"Charlotte Raines."

His deep brown eyes slid back to me. They were barely visible underneath his blue police hat.

"No, that would be my sister." I let out a deep sigh.

"Tell him you are here for the file in the top drawer with your name on it." Charlotte appeared next to me.

"I'm here to get the file my sister left for me with my name on it in the top drawer." I pointed behind me. God, I hoped there was a file in that top drawer with my name on it. My heart thumped. My palms were sweating.

"Are you really going to go in there and look?" the receptionist cried from the door when the officer walked into the office.

"Do you smell him?" Charlotte's face lit up. "He's dreamy."

Charlotte stood next to him with her eyes closed and breathing deeply the scent of the man. She was right. He did smell good.

"What is going on here?" Gina Marie Hardgrove stood behind the receptionist. Her beady eyes snapped at me.

"That woman trespassed, locked the door and did God knows what in here while I told her that Ms. Raines was on vacation. So I called the police." The woman's chin lifted up and then down.

"Officer." Gina walked in; she didn't bother looking at me. She simply folded her hands in front of her body, the big diamond ring glistening. "I'm sure my receptionist overreacted." She lifted her arm and curled her hand around mine, giving it a good, tight squeeze that was enough for me to know she wasn't pleased, but gentle enough for me not to scream. "Emma Lee and I have been friends a long time. I'm sure there's a reasonable explanation for her behavior." She dropped her hand. "In fact, Emma is sick." She curled her nose and looked at me. "Isn't that right, Emma?"

The officer's hand was on the drawer. My eyes begged him to open it. I really wanted to know if there was a file in there for me and if the file was her signature on a duplicate contract since she ripped up the other one.

It would be just like Charlotte to be dramatic and rip up a contract when she knew there was another one in her desk.

"She takes medicine for the 'Funeral Trauma.'" Gina Marie Hardgrove did something that made me want to deck her right there. She circled her forefinger around her ear like I was crazy.

"Yes. I'm Emma Lee Raines, Charlotte's sister." I held my head high. "I do have 'Funeral Trauma.'"

I guess acting crazy in order not to get arrested

was my best bet when Gina Marie was giving me a pass on trespassing. Or she knew I was there because Charlotte was dead and she wanted to see what I knew.

"Well." The officer dropped his hand from the drawer handle and my heart sank into my toes. Grief and despair tore me up inside. I couldn't help but hope there was a file in there with my name. "If the two of you can work this out, it would be best."

"Yes, officer." Gina nodded. "Isn't that right, Emma?"

"Yes," I whispered, wanting to protest, but it was best to keep my mouth shut.

"You don't have 'Funeral Trauma'!" Charlotte screamed. "Tell them! Tell them!"

Silently I stood as the officer walked out of Charlotte's office. The receptionist huffed off, leaving me there with Gina Marie.

When the coast was clear, Gina took the moment.

"So you thought you could come in here while your sister is on vacation and see if you can take some of her clients like you broke into Burns and took their clients?" Gina's hands were planted on her hips.

"Who said I did that?" I protested.

It was true that I'd broken into Burns Funeral to

get Mamie's teeth out of her file like Charlotte Rae had asked me about earlier, but no way in hell was I trying to take their clients.

"Charlotte told me all about your little crazy tricks." Gina's chest heaved up when she took a deep breath and down when she let it out.

"I . . ." Charlotte started to explain. "I had no idea that those crazy stunts were because you can see the dead. I mean"—her voice faded—"I'm so sorry."

"I wasn't trying to steal anything." I glared at Gina Marie.

Now I wished I had been arrested.

There was no doubt in my mind that she was going to run a smear campaign against me and the funeral home.

"I think it's best you leave and let your sister deal with you when she gets back." Gina walked to the office door and pointed for me to leave.

"If my sister is on vacation, then why is her car here?" I asked and walked out into the hallway.

"She went with Sammy. They left from here." Gina Marie slammed Charlotte's door between us.

"You could've told me about Sammy Hardgrove and this vacation," I whispered when Charlotte wisped on by me on our way out of Hardgrove's. I gave jazz fingers to the receptionist. "Toodles."

She glared.

I had to remind myself that it didn't matter what should've been done; Charlotte Rae was dead. My entire body literally stopped functioning. My feet stopped working. The muscles in my face stopped working because as much as I tried to pick my jaw up off the sidewalk in front of the fountain, my mouth wouldn't close. My gut tugged.

"Charlotte," I gasped after I got my lungs to suck in some air and out my mouth. "Either Sammy Hardgrove or his wife killed you."

"Sammy boy wouldn't do that." The words oozed out of her mouth, giving me an ick factor all over my body. "But his wife," Charlotte snapped. "That's another story."

"Sammy boy?" I sucked in a deep breath and shook my head. "You know I have to call Jack Henry."

"You can't do that," Charlotte begged. "Then the whole world would know."

I put my hand over my brow to shield my eyes from the sun. The police officer was standing on the sidewalk talking to Arley and Hardgrove's security guard. Arley leaned on the metal rake and the security guard was in a golf cart.

"Crap." My heart sank when I saw Arley still holding the files in his hands.

Not that they'd do me any good since I was about one hundred percent sure Charlotte was offed by a bitter wife, and the woman had dumped Charlotte somewhere.

But where?

Arley and the officer shook hands and the officer got in his cruiser and left before I got to the hearse. Arley still had the files. The security guard zipped away in the golf cart, but not without giving me a good stare.

"Ms. Emma." Arley handed the files to me.

"What was he talking about?" I had to know. Especially if it was about me.

"He told me and our security guard to keep an eye out for you if you tried to come back and to not let you in." He pointed to the files. "What do you want with those?"

"Charlotte called me from vacation and asked me to give a couple people follow-up calls." I smiled through my lie. "I'm only doing it for her so Gina won't fire her for not tying up loose ends before she went on vacation." I opened the hearse door and threw the files on the seat. "Say, Arley, did you ever see Sammy with Charlotte?"

"Um." He stuck his finger in his mouth and gnawed on the side of the tip by his nail.

"By the sounds of your um, you did." It didn't take a lie detector to tell me Arley was hiding something. "What is going on around here?"

"Ms. Emma, you and John Howard have a

good relationship and I'm sure he sees things he shouldn't and doesn't say a word. It's a lot of the same around here. I can't say a word. I have a family. A new baby and a stack of unpaid medical bills for my daddy. I have to have my job."

Arley was right. I had to respect his employment.

"I'm sorry. Congratulations on the new baby." A wry smile crossed my lips. "I'm sorry to hear about your dad. Is he okay?"

"Nah. He got that lung thing from smoking all these years." Arley's voice faded away.

"COPD?" I asked. The hurt he was feeling radiated through his body.

He nodded. His eyes sad. "He's on oxygen all the time. So forgive me if I can't gossip or tell things that aren't related to me. I have a family to look out for."

"I'm sorry I put you in that position. I completely understand and Charlotte was very lucky to have an employee like you." I couldn't help but think about my relationship with John Howard and hoped he'd do the same for me if he were put in a similar situation.

"Was?" Arley's brows furrowed. "Am I getting fired?"

"Oh no." A nervous giggle escaped me. "She's very lucky to have an employee like you."

"But you said was." Arley sure did have a good memory.

"Did I?" I asked and jumped into the hearse before he could ask any more questions. "Thanks for the help."

"All right." He nodded and stared at me the entire time I backed up and pulled out of Hardgrove's.

"He sure is a nice man." Charlotte sat in the front seat.

"Was there really a file in your top drawer for me?" I asked.

"Yes. There is," Charlotte confirmed. "But I'm begging you. Please don't tell Jack Henry anything until you figure out if Mary Katherine Hardgrove killed me. Let's find my body, then we can tell him." Charlotte's lip jutted out. She put her hands together in a prayer pose. "Please. I don't want people to remember me in death with a Charlotte letter." She snorted. An un-Charlotte thing to do. She stuck her elbow out. "Get it? Charlotte letter. Scarlet letter?"

"Yeah. I get it." Though I didn't find it too funny that she was making a mockery of the fact she was the other woman. Never in a million decades would I have thought Charlotte would've stooped to such a low level. It wasn't her standards. And to think it was with a Hardgrove. Sammy Hardgrove to be exact.

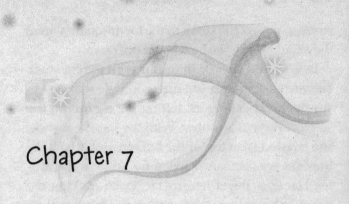

Chapter 7

There wasn't time to pay Sammy and Mary Katherine Hardgrove a visit before Sissy Phillips's funeral. I feared I was going to be late as it was, since the police officer took up more time than I had allowed.

"Aren't we going to find me?" Charlotte spat.

"No. We are going to put Sissy in the ground." I gripped the wheel and zoomed back to Sleepy Hollow.

Sissy's cousin, Bess Phillips, was standing on the front porch smoking her big cig, giving me the stink eye when I pulled up. She damn good and well knew that I didn't allow smoking on the property. There was even a nice sign that I had made and nailed to the brick by the door that directed smokers across the street to the town square where they could sit on the bench and puff away.

Bess's hand curved in the air with the cig stuck between her thumb and finger. On the way down, she opened her fingers, letting the cig fall on the steps of Eternal Slumber. With the toe of her shoe, she twisted it on top of the burning tobacco until the butt was smashed like a fly hit by a flyswatter. Her eyes never left my face once, making me believe she'd done that exact same move a time or two.

"I've got a bone to pick with you, Emma Lee Raines." The creases around her lips, caused from entirely too much sunbathing, deepened as she duck-billed them together.

Whatever bone Bess had to pick with me had to wait. I could see there were already people in the foyer of the funeral home ready to view Sissy's body and pay their respects.

"Did you hear me, Emma Lee Raines?" Bess stood next to the hearse with her hands planted on her thin waist, her hip jutted to the right. Her newly permed hair was entirely too tight and I wondered if Mary Anna Hardy was losing her touch. "You've done went and lost our family pin. Our heirloom. We told you that we wanted that pin stuck right here." Bess smacked her boob so hard, it hurt me.

"Bess, calm down." I assured her.

"She's backwoods crazy." Charlotte noted something we already knew about that family.

"I did give Mary Anna the clothes and pin you gave me. I told her your strict instructions and she repeated them back to me." I walked past her. "If the pin isn't there, I'm sure it's with your belongings I need to give back to you."

After one of our loved ones goes to their final eternity and their family entrusts them into my care, I ask for things like photos to put together a memory collage for the DVD and have a television set up near the signing book for the line of mourners to watch as they wait. I also get a collection of the deceased's favorite music, which we piped through the dinosaur intercom. Sissy's just so happened to be the heavy metal eighties rock group Metallica. When I tried to steer Bess, Sissy's beneficiary, away from such music, she wouldn't hear of it.

The thrashing metal hit, "Master Of Puppets," was crackling through the speakers. Granny stood by the signing book. Her head was ticking toward the viewing room. I wasn't sure if she was trying to tell me something or about to head bang. I just never knew with her. When her lip twitched, I knew she was wanting me to look in the viewing room. James, Bess's brother, was playing air guitar right next to Sissy's head. When our eyes caught, he gave me the rock 'n' roll sign with his fingers and stuck his tongue out while shaking his pointy Mohawk back and forth.

"Have you seen Mary Anna?" I asked Granny.

"This is a disgrace to our family business and the dead." Granny's displeasure was written on her face.

"What are you gonna do about my family heirloom?" Bess said through her brown gritted teeth. The nicotine oozed from her pores.

"I'll be right back." I punched the down button on the elevator, the only button for the elevator, and stepped in, enjoying the quiet on my short trip downstairs.

Vernon wasn't in the morgue, Mary Anna hadn't come to pay her respects and there was not an alumni pin anywhere to be found.

"Where is it?" I asked, practically tearing the place apart looking for it.

"You'll find it." Charlotte stood next to the elevator.

"You scared me to death." I held my hands to my heart.

"I have to talk to you." Charlotte walked over and just watched me opening drawers and scouring through them. "I need you to promise me you won't say anything to Jack Henry."

"Only if you can help." I shook my head. It was just like Charlotte to never pitch in. Ever. "I have to get upstairs before Granny or Bess goes nuts." I held the elevator door. "Are you coming or not?"

Charlotte shook her head. "I just don't want to see Granny right now knowing the pain she's going to be in when she finds out about me . . ." Charlotte didn't finish her sentence. She simply dragged her finger across her throat.

"Fine." I pulled my hand away and let the elevator door close between us. My mind reeled on where the pin could be. Mary Anna had left the clothing bag downstairs along with the file, which is where she should've left it, but there was no pin. I vividly remembered a pin was in there too. And my only hope was to get in touch with Mary Anna to find out if she knew where it was.

The elevator doors slid open to a vestibule full of Sleepy Hollow residents. My heart nearly leapt out of my chest when I saw Bea Allen Burns. Seeing Bea Allen made me cringe. It would give her great pleasure if she found out that we were missing Sissy's pin.

"Nice turnout, Emma Lee." Bea Allen's brow rose a trifle as she approached me.

"Thank you." I smiled and for a split second I wanted to ask her about Peggy Wayne's pearls, but decided to put that card in my back pocket.

Bess saw me and made a beeline toward us. I quickly darted down the hall to find Mary Anna.

"Did you put Sissy's pin on her? Right here?" I asked when I found her in the kitchen making a pot of coffee.

"Of course I did. Her cousin, Bess, you know the one who ate supper before grace"—Mary Anna's eyebrows lifted in the gossip way—"she made sure it was put on Sissy."

"You mean to tell me little Joey was born out of wedlock?" My jaw dropped after hearing the (apparently) old news about Bess and Matt Previs's child. It was news to me since I didn't gossip. Much.

"Sure was." Mary Anna flipped the coffee-maker on.

"The pin is not there," I stated.

"Not there?" Mary Anna asked. "I know I put it on her."

Bea Allen walked in and pretended to get a coffee mug while she was eavesdropping. The look on her face told me she was enjoying this little slip-up.

"Did you find the pin?" Bess popped her head in the kitchen with an unlit cig hanging out of her mouth. "It's almost time, Emma Lee."

"Mary Anna assures me she put it on her chest just like Sissy wanted." I knew there was no excuse in the world that would make up for this big mistake. "I know there is sentimental value to the family heirloom and I will find it before the burial."

"I did put it on there," Mary Anna huffed, pushing me aside. "I'll show you."

All of us followed Mary Anna to the viewing room.

She marched right on up to the casket and hovered over it like Sissy was down on her makeup table in the basement, while the rest of us stood in the doorway of the viewing room.

"I'm telling you it was right here! You can see the hole!" she screamed from the front and pointed at poor Sissy's dead body over top of the screeching Metallica.

The entire room fell silent until a giggle came from the corner of the viewing room. The giggle turned into laughter and then an all-out guffaw. I didn't have to look to know exactly who was taking pleasure in my pain. Charlotte Rae Raines.

I marched up to the casket with everyone's eyes on me alongside Bess. Mary Anna was still jutting her finger toward the pin hole. She was right. The hole was there, but the pin was not.

I slid my head toward Charlotte and glared, hoping she'd stop laughing. The entire crowd looked at me as if waiting to see how I was going to handle this situation. On one side of the room I had Mary Anna screaming about the pin and on the opposite side was a hysterical Charlotte enjoying my misfortune.

To make matters worse, that darn tabby cat was standing right on top of Sissy's casket.

I turned to face Mary Anna and tried to shoo the cat away with my hand so no one would see. The cat didn't move. It just kept staring at Sissy.

"Scat," I whispered under my breath.

"Well, I never." Mary Anna drew back, stuck her fingers in her hair and fluffed it up before she turned on her heels and faced the crowd.

Granny shuffled up the aisle and greeted a few people on her way. It was her way to break up the tension in the room. She whispered a few things to Bess, who then took her spot up front with Sissy's other kinfolk. Then Granny put her magic touch on Mary Anna, who shuffled the other way.

"The cat!" Charlotte screamed and pointed. The darn cat was curled up in the crook of Sissy's stiff arm.

"Scat!" I screamed and shooed, trying to get the cat to scram. The cat got up, stretched, and jumped out of the casket and strolled down the aisle and out the door just as Jack Henry was coming into the vestibule.

"Emma Lee." Granny took me by the arm. "Are you feeling okay?"

Jack Henry's eyes met mine. There was concern on his face.

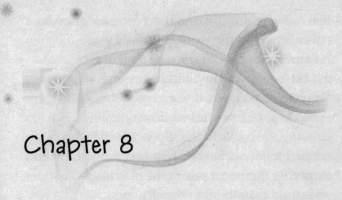

Chapter 8

Sissy's funeral went off without a hitch according to her family, minus the pin.

Bess had come to terms that the pin was missing. She really settled down after I gave her fifty percent off the casket. It was a big chunk to take off, but a big mistake was made. I did assure her that we would try to find the pin. She did say that she didn't put it past one of the family members to have stolen the pin off "poor old Sissy's dead body" because there was a rift—which was a nice way of saying a fight—in the family over the pin being buried with her.

I couldn't rule out what Bess had said about the pin because an hour before the community viewing, I had allowed the family to view the body in private like I always do. Out of respect for their grieving, I never stayed in the room unless they asked. Whoever took it had an hour to slip it off of her.

"You seemed to be a little more emotional about Sissy than you usually are with your other clients." Jack Henry walked down the line of chairs untying the backs of the slipcovers in the viewing room. I followed behind him taking them off and throwing them in a pile in the middle of the room so I could take them to the cleaners.

"Death just seems to be lingering." I wasn't sure how to approach the subject with him about that cat. "Keep an eye out for the pin, please." I pointed to the carpet.

"Okay." Jack's voice faded, losing its steely edge. His eyes bore into me. He knew I was keeping something from him, but let me keep it to myself. "Did you see anyone lingering a little too close to the corpse?"

"Not that I can recall." I shrugged and threw more of the chair covers on the pile for the dry cleaners. We have a written contract where they come and pick up the linens after each service. It helps me out a lot.

"Emma." Jack Henry stood by the chair next to the window that overlooked the town square and a direct view of the Sleepy Hollow Inn. "The inn."

My eyes slid over to the window and out at the blue flashing lights.

My heart stopped. I stopped and gripped the top of the folding chair with a fist full of linen.

"Oh my God. They found her." I gulped.

"Emma Lee." Jack stared at me. Our eyes met. I tried to swallow, only my mouth felt like it was filled with sand. "You are going to have to act surprised."

Without thinking, I dropped the slipcover and ran as fast as I could out of the funeral home, down the concrete steps, and across the street without looking for cars passing by. The newly born spring grass lifted me as I raced across the town square, darting around the gazebo. In the distance, under the light of the inn's front porch carriage lights, I could see two Lexington police officers standing on the porch talking to Granny. Charlotte Rae was standing next to her.

"Granny!" I screamed, waving my hands in the dark night. "Granny!" Running faster than I ever had. It was like time stood still when I reached the porch.

My eyes clung to hers, trying to measure her reaction. A rare and primitive grief crossed Granny's face.

"Sir." I grabbed Granny. She buried her head in my neck. "I'm Emma Lee Raines. Charlotte's sister."

"We are so sorry to inform you about your sister's death." The tallest of the two officers held his hat to his chest. His eyes caught mine. His eyes lowered. "You are the intruder . . ."

Crap. He was the same officer who had come to Hardgrove's and warned me not to come back.

"Ahem." Jack cleared his throat. I didn't have to look at him to know that he'd caught on to the tail end of the officer's admission of seeing me earlier. Something I had yet to tell him about, though I might never have told him.

"Do you know who murdered her?" I asked, hoping to get this solved as quickly as possible. I wasn't sure how Granny would hold up if I had to investigate her murder myself.

"Who said she was murdered?" the smaller and beefier officer asked. He had questioning eyes. "We aren't sure she didn't commit suicide."

"Murdered? Suicide?" Granny sobbed in the crook of my neck. "There is no way she would have committed suicide."

"Suicide!" Charlotte was just as stunned as me. "No way. I was murdered, Emma Lee. Tell them!" The shrill Charlotte voice I was used to was back. "Tell them now!" The bossy Charlotte I was used to was back. "If you don't tell them, I will haunt you forever and it won't be pleasant."

"Suicide?" The word dripped out of my mouth like a curse word. "There is no way Charlotte would ever commit suicide. She is way too conceited."

"Emma Lee!" Granny gasped, switching from

my neck to Jack Henry's. Whoever was going to comfort her the way she wanted, she was going to.

"I'm Sheriff Ross, the sheriff here in Sleepy Hollow." Jack shook hands with both officers. "Please, come in. As you can see, we are in a bit of shock."

The officers seemed to be more interested in me than the fact my sister had been murdered.

Jack Henry opened the door and the officers walked in the foyer of the inn.

"Emma, what's going on?" Cheryl Lynne Doyle, still wearing the Higher Grounds apron, stood on the sidewalk in front of the inn with the rest of Sleepy Hollow. "We saw the flashing lights." She gestured behind her.

"Charlotte Rae has been ki—" The word killed almost escaped my lips. "Has died." My head lowered along with my voice.

An audible gasp blanketed the crowd as I headed inside. Right behind me came Hettie Bell.

"Don't worry about the inn." She grabbed me by my shoulders. "I'm here as long as Zula needs me. I'm not busy at Pose and Relax anyways."

Immediately, Hettie took over and spoke to the guests staying at the inn who had gathered in the foyer to see what was going on. I turned right into the gathering room where Granny kept snack foods and held high-noon tea for her guests.

Sadly, there was nothing but a display of empty dishes. By the looks of Granny and the flour in her hair and on her face, she had been preparing for the next day's menu when the officers arrived.

"Ma'am." The officer turned his attention to me. Jack had seated Granny on the couch, but didn't let go of her. He was a great pillar of strength and Granny needed it right now. "Why do you think your sister was murdered?"

"I . . ." Out of the corner of my eye, Jack Henry's head drifted toward the ground. He knew. "This would be out of character for Charlotte. There is no way she would do this to herself or us."

"Her boyfriend found her in his apartment on the south side of Lexington with an empty bottle of pills in her grip." The officer read off a small notepad.

Granny's little body couldn't take any more. Jack Henry laid her completely down on the couch and knelt down next to her. Granny lifted her hand over her eyes; her body shook with pain before she darted up.

"Her boyfriend?" Granny growled. Her blood-shot eyes narrowed as she spoke. "Charlotte didn't have a boyfriend. Are you sure you are talking about my granddaughter, Charlotte Rae Raines?"

Oh no. Just another layer of Charlotte that Granny was going to be upset about. I warned

Charlotte that when Granny found out about Sammy, she'd go bat-shit crazy.

"Yes, ma'am." The shorter officer kept his eyes on me while answering Granny's question. "We have a statement from Mr. Samuel Hardgrove who identified her."

"Sammy Hardgrove found her?" Immediately he became a suspect right along with his wife.

"Samuel Hardgrove is married. You are mistaken." Granny shook her head. Her red hair was no longer styled neatly.

"No, ma'am, we are not mistaken." The officer was being a complete jerk. "Maybe there was a side of your granddaughter she didn't want you to see."

"That is enough!" I bolted into his face. "You can leave now."

When the officer stuck his hand on the butt of his gun that was snapped into his hip holster, Jack Henry popped up to his feet and got between me and the officer.

"Thank you for coming by. As you can tell, this has been a blow to the family." Jack Henry and the cop had their cop thing going on with the looks. They weren't fooling me any. "Can you give us the rest of the day to digest what has happened? Zula can come by to work out the details for the body after the autopsy is done."

"I don't see a problem with that, do you?" the

officer asked the other. "Let's leave these good people to grieve."

"We are sorry for your loss," the officers said in unison before they let themselves out.

There was a brief silence. Each of us seemed to wait to see if the other was going to break the stillness between us.

"Granny," I whispered. "I'm sure there is an explanation for this. I really don't think Charlotte committed suicide."

Granny's chin lifted. There was a scowl full of piss and vinegar on her face.

"There is one thing I do know." Granny lifted herself to stand. "Charlotte would never be caught dead in public without makeup on. So, there is no way she would let her legacy be left to a suicide." She shook her finger at Jack Henry. "Someone murdered my granddaughter and you are going to figure out who did it."

"That's right, Granny!" Charlotte clapped her hands in delight. "You keep that attitude." Charlotte beamed like Granny could hear her.

"Heaven help the fool that wronged her." Granny shook her head before she hung it back toward the ground and shuffled out of the room and up the stairs.

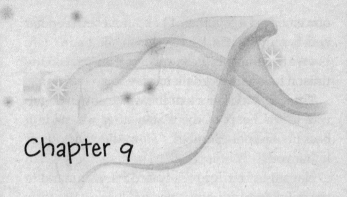

Chapter 9

Hettie Bell talked Granny into drinking one of her lime-green concoctions after I had slipped in a couple of sleeping pills to knock Granny out cold.

The inn was going to be filled with people coming and going, dropping off food and giving their condolences, and Granny just wasn't up to it.

When someone died, the Auxiliary women went to work and ordered all the residents to bake something or buy something to take to the deceased's family's home. Generally, Granny was in charge of this task, but not this time.

There wasn't a dry eye at the inn when I left. Everyone loved Charlotte Rae. She was always the pretty one, the sane one, the best-dressed one, the one who had it together. The scandal between her and Sammy was a legacy I wish she hadn't left. But with Sammy as the number one suspect on my radar, I knew I was going to have to go see him.

"Spill it." Jack Henry didn't waste any time getting to the heart of the matter after we made it back to Eternal Slumber. "How did that officer know you?"

"I went to Hardgrove's before Sissy's funeral to see if I could find any clues in Charlotte's office. The receptionist called the police to report me trespassing, but Gina Marie covered for me."

"When I asked you to turn around and let my buddy on the force handle it, you actually lied?" he asked with a slightly tilted head.

"Not lied, just kept out every detail of what I was doing." Of course it was a lie. I knew he wasn't going to go along with me wanting to go back up to Hardgrove's when we both assumed Charlotte's death had something to do with that place.

"No matter how big or small, a lie is a lie." Jack took the moral high ground, the one that made him such a great cop.

"I did find out a bit of information that you can look into." Changing the subject off me was exactly where this conversation needed to go.

"Like what?" he asked.

"Charlotte was going on vacation with Sammy. She and Sammy were having an affair." I put my fisted palm in the other palm and grinded it. "I have never been so mad in my life."

The ghost cat darted into the room and jumped up next to Jack Henry. Immediately he started to sneeze and scratch his nose. The cat dragged its tail under Jack Henry's chin as it walked across Jack Henry's lap. He reached up and scratched.

"Are you okay?" I asked and put my hand on his shoulder as he sneezed.

His eyes squinted, his nose curled, and his mouth slightly opened before he sneezed again.

"I haven't sneezed like this since I was a kid and found out I was allergic to cats." He put his face in his hands and sneezed a few more times.

"Oh no." I couldn't help myself. I brought my hands up to stifle my giggles. "I hate to tell you but there is a ghost cat following me around."

"What?" Jack Henry jumped up and rubbed his hands through his hair. "Your sister and a cat?" I gave him a sympathetic look and made a kissy face. "Are they related?"

"No, but . . ." I stopped to remember Sissy's missing pin. I had heard cats loved to play with shiny things. Had the cat taken the pin?

"Huh?" Jack shook his head.

"The cat was all curled up on Sissy. Do you think it could've eaten the pin?" I questioned.

"Anything is possible around here," he said. "I guess you are going to have to look around. Don't ghosts move stuff all the time?"

"I guess." I shrugged. "Charlotte said the cat isn't attached to her. So I wonder if he was attached to someone else here and is just now finding me." I shook my head. "It's obviously not my top priority. Let me get you some allergy medicine."

I went into my kitchenette and rummaged through the drawers. There wasn't any there.

"Look in my office bathroom. I have some in the cabinet." Charlotte appeared out of nowhere, causing me to jump. "You two really are cute, Emma."

"Thanks." I headed out the door. "Charlotte said she had some in her office bathroom."

"She did, did she?" Jack Henry paced back and forth, scratching his nose. It was beet-red. "Ask her who killed her."

I hurried out into the funeral home and went directly to the bathroom, finding the medicine exactly where she said it was. I hadn't even thought about cleaning out the bathroom when I took over.

"She doesn't know," I called over my shoulder when I walked back into the kitchenette and grabbed a beer out of the small refrigerator and took it to Jack. "Or I would've already told you."

"Thank you," Jack said through a stuffy nose and took the meds, swigging them down with the beer. "Is she here now?" He sat down on the couch.

I looked around. "No." I sat down next to him, pulling my feet up under my legs and resting my head on Jack Henry's shoulder. I laid my hand on his chest. It felt so safe. "She is dirty. There is dirt on her suit, and you and I both know Charlotte Rae never got dirty. And if she did, she immediately cleaned herself up."

"I'm worried about you. You seem awfully calm for someone who has just lost her sister." His warm breath hit my skull along with a pair of very soft lips.

"It doesn't seem real because I can see and talk to her." My heart felt a little tug from the knowledge that when I did help her cross over, I would have to deal with the fact I wouldn't see her again. "She's actually much nicer in death."

"Probably because she needs you to help her." Jack made a good point. "Not that she didn't need you before. I didn't like the way she treated you when she was here. Did she say anything about the papers?"

"Not really. She said there is a file with my

name on it in her top drawer." I bit my lip thinking about Charlotte's face after Granny's reaction when the cops told her that Sammy Hardgrove had identified Charlotte's body. I'd never seen such pain in her eyes. Eyes were so haunting. "She begged me not to say anything to you about the affair because she didn't want people to know."

"Unfortunately, that will be the last thing they remember about her." Jack ran his hand up and down my back. "You're thinking the wife found out?"

"That was what Charlotte was worried about. I can't help but wonder if Mary Katherine Hardgrove found out about her husband's affair and killed Charlotte in a fit of rage."

"I'm hoping the Lexington police changed Charlotte's death to a homicide and turned the case over. I should hear any minute from my buddy and then you can get her body home where it belongs." Jack was trying to soothe me, but the only thing on my mind was getting Charlotte's killer.

"Maybe I can dig around until then. I know the Hardgroves pretty well." I should've told Jack Henry about the files I had taken from Charlotte's office, but I didn't have the energy to explain it. Any energy I had left, I wanted to focus on him.

"I really don't want you to do that." Jack pulled back and I looked up at him. "I'm thinking you are just going to have to put up with her ghost until the Lexington police figure it out."

His mouth moved over mine, devouring every bit of softness before he crushed me to him, picking me up. Slowly he walked with me nestled in his arms, his lips seared down my neck. I squinted with one eye open. With that one eye, I scanned the room, making sure there was no sign of Charlotte or that cat.

When I saw the coast was clear, I threw both arms around Jack Henry's neck and let him help me forget the day's pain.

Chapter 10

"Wake up, sleepyhead." The voice curled around me, bringing me out of my slumber.

The sunlight pierced my eyelids, waking my mind to the events of the day that lay ahead. Things I never wanted to ever be part of. It meant I was going to have to get up and look Jack Henry in the eyes—after a night I wouldn't forget in a long time—and lie straight to his face, even smile while doing it.

There was a heaviness on my chest. It wasn't the loss of Charlotte, it was the darn cat all curled up and sleeping on me.

I put my arms above my head and stretched to high heavens before opening my eyes. The cat jumped up and darted off the bed.

"Charlotte." I looked to the left of me at the empty space and the neatly pulled up covers where I knew Jack was lying a few short hours ago.

"Wake up, sleepyhead." She giggled and twiddled her fingers my way. "I reckon you thought I was Jack about to send you sweet nothings?" She sat down on the edge of the bed. "You don't have time to lollygag around here. We've got a murder to solve, starting with Mary Katherine Hardgrove."

I glanced over at my clock.

"It's seven"—I rolled back over and pulled the covers over my head—"in the morning. I'm sure Mary Katherine is not even out of bed yet."

"Oh yes she is. I know for a fact that she goes every morning at seven to Stevon's on Rose to get a seaweed facial."

I sat up and looked at her.

"What are you thinking?" I asked in a shaky voice wondering what she was up to.

"Sammy and I were supposed to be on vacation in the Virgin Islands. He told Mary Katherine he had a funeral conference in Des Moines." She stood up and walked into the small entryway where I had a mirror hanging on the wall. She ran her hands down her long red hair and brushed at the dirt spots a couple of times. "My last morning with Sammy, we made love a couple of times and enjoyed breakfast in bed before I headed to the office to work until it was time for us to meet up."

"Oh." My ick factor went off and made my nose curl. "I just can't believe you were having an affair with a married man, especially him."

Sammy and Dale Hardgrove. Both gross. Sammy the worst one. There was no doubt in my mind that he seduced Charlotte. He was always sniffing around her like a dog. Dale did too, but Sammy was much more aggressive. One time when my parents had taken us to a funeral conference in Las Vegas, I caught Sammy and Charlotte wrestling tongues in the kid's video game room. I've never been able to play "Ms. Pac-Man" since.

"Mary Katherine takes advantage of him and he told me so." Charlotte lifted her chin in the air and slightly turned it away from me.

"Fine." I threw the covers off of me and grabbed my robe out of my closet on my way to the bathroom. "I'm not here to judge you. I'm here to figure out who killed you. So it looks like I'm going to get a seaweed facial."

The long hot shower didn't make the ache of losing Charlotte go away, but it did wake me up. While Charlotte waited, I got dressed in jeans and a sweatshirt. I figured I'd be spending the day at the inn after I got back from Stevon's. Granny was going to need me and so would my parents.

Jack had left a note on the table by the door in the entry of my small apartment. He wanted me to call him when I got up. What he didn't know didn't hurt him. I could always blame it on grief. Seriously, what did he expect? It was my sister.

For a split second I thought I might grab a coffee from Higher Grounds, but I didn't want anyone asking questions about Charlotte.

It wasn't long until I had the hearse pulled up to the curve on Rose Lane, right in front of Stevon's on Rose. Stevon's was like most businesses in this area, small cottage-style homes that have been turned into high-end shops.

"May I help you?" The man with slicked-back gray hair, skintight black pants, flip-flops with toes manicured better than mine and a tight black V-neck short-sleeved knit top greeted me as soon as I opened the door, his man-scaped brows cocked. He lifted his chin, his eyes drew down his nose and he stared at me. He hugged an iPad in his hand.

"I would like to get a seaweed wrap." I smiled and looked behind him in what looked like it used to be a family room. A head with a white towel twisted up on her head peeked over the back of the couch that faced a glowing fireplace.

"Facial," Charlotte quickly corrected me.

"I mean facial." I smiled.

"Okay." Dramatically the man lifted his finger in the air, at shoulder length, and curved it down on the iPad, poking away. "I can get you in this time next year."

"Next year?" I noticed his unresponsiveness to my are-you-joking-me tone.

Charlotte rushed into the room with the fireplace. The flames blew out. The woman on the couch turned around and looked at me and the man.

"That's her!" Charlotte pointed. "Killer!"

I gulped and smiled at the man.

"Yes, next year." He didn't budge a smile or a frown. His face was stone cold stiff, along with his eyes. "One moment."

He set the iPad on the small table next to the door and scurried over to re-light the electric logs in the fireplace.

"I'm so sorry, Mrs. Hardgrove," he profusely apologized.

"Un, un." Charlotte shimmied a little as she stood over the iPad and used her finger to poke, swipe and type. "Now tell him that you have an appointment today."

"I had an appointment today." My voice was less than assuring.

"No." His face pruned. "I don't think so." He crossed his skinny arms in front of him. His eyes slid to the door.

"Tell him to look again," Charlotte demanded.

"Can you just look one more time?" I asked nicely. "Please?"

He let out a long huff and did that swiping routine with his finger. While he looked for my name, I noticed there were two changing rooms on the left, a hallway and the room where Mrs. Hardgrove was relaxing.

He blinked a couple of times. His lashes flew open. He looked at me with surprise.

"Emma Lee Raines?" His voice faded to a hushed stillness. "It can't be." He looked again. "I'm sorry, Ms. Raines. I must've looked at the wrong day. We only have one client room with two clients a day. I have had the same two clients every morning, but it's Stevon's shop." He flung his wrist in the air, before he pointed me to the door behind us. "You will find a robe on the back of the door and a fresh linen. When you have the robe on, you can come out here by the fireplace with Mrs. Hardgrove."

"Mrs. Hardgrove." Charlotte spit like the name put a bad taste in her mouth.

I smiled politely and disappeared into the changing room before whoever was supposed to be here got there and I was kicked out.

The clean, fresh spa smell was being pumped out from the floor vent. I had always wondered how a spa perpetually smelled like that. The room was all white. The furniture was all white, a bed, a chair and end table. The bed was covered in white linens and the chair had a white throw over the back. There was a fuzzy white rug in the center of the room. The bathroom was completely done in white tile, with a white claw-foot tub, and a clear glass bowl on top of a white wash sink.

"You are going to love the new mask this morning. There is a touch of peppermint added to the seaweed." The male voice was a bit muffled and drifted up under the crack of the shut door. "I was surprised to see you had missed yesterday. It's not like you." His voice escalated.

I opened the door just a crack to make sure he was talking to Mary Katherine and when I saw it was only the two of them, I could confirm that Mary Katherine had missed her appointment yesterday morning. Not that it placed her killing Charlotte—it hadn't because Charlotte was killed after I had seen her later in the morning—but it did confirm that Mary had missed her standing appointment here at Stevon's.

I walked over to the bed where there was a white robe and fresh linen neatly folded. I took my clothes off and put them in the bin, and put on the robe as he instructed. I felt a little odd going out to the room and sitting down next to

Charlotte's killer. I might've been putting the cart before the horse, but everything added up for her to kill my sister.

I took a deep breath, telling myself to keep my composure, and walked out of the room.

"Hi," I said to Mary Katherine when I reached the couch.

I sat down next to her where a small bowl of water was placed on the floor next to her small bowl of water. I mimicked Mary Katherine and put my feet in the water. Her head was leaned against the back of the couch, so I leaned my head exactly like her. Her hands were crossed in her lap and so did I. Finally, I closed my eyes like her. She never breathed a word.

I had never seen her before. She had pale white skin, pink full lips, black thick lashes. She was a very attractive woman. For a second I wondered why on earth Sammy Hardgrove would cheat on her. She did look a little like porcelain, which was usually cold to the touch, so maybe he was looking for Charlotte to warm him. Who knew? But I was here to get some answers and get out.

"Go on, ask her." Charlotte was crouched down in front of Mary Katherine in a position I'd never thought I'd see Charlotte in. "Or just tell her that you know she killed me."

"Good morning, ladies." A large round woman

with a heavy German accent greeted us with a big glass bowl of green slimy-looking leaves piled together. Mary Katherine stayed still, so I followed, keeping one eye open for good measure.

The woman stood behind the couch and reached around with a long piece of seaweed in her hand. She stuck it to Mary Katherine's face in a circle, grabbing more and more seaweed.

When it came to my turn, I tried to close my eyes, but the smell of the seaweed about burned my nose hairs. It was so foul.

"Good golly." I jumped up, flinging the damp pieces of seaweed against the fireplace. They stuck for a second before sliding down the wall and landing with a faint smack.

"I've never." The German woman gasped, placing her large man hands on her big boobs. "I will not work with you." She stomped out of the room.

I looked around. The man was gone from the front and Mary Katherine didn't budge. Still stone. I leaned over and put my finger under her nose to see if I could feel any air coming out, because she was as still as a corpse.

"I'm alive." Mary Katherine's lips moved and I jumped back. "I'm just curious to know why you are here when I know that Clarice Thompson is supposed to be here. You see . . ." Mary Katherine tilted her face down and turned it toward me.

The piece of seaweed on her forehead fell into her lap. "Clarice and I are best friends. We talk every morning before our treatment." Her green eyes bore into me. "So what is it that you wanted to know about me? Are you my husband's lover? Are you the one that is supposed to go to the Virgin Islands with him and he dumped your sorry, plain-Jane ass? Because believe me, I looked at you when you came in, and you must be a good lay because you sure couldn't hold a candle to me." She brought her hand up to her face and looked at her fingernails. She had one of those big diamond rings on her finger. There were enough *carrots* on her finger to feed a pasture full of horses. "Honey, he told me all about it last night when he was groveling for forgiveness. Begging me to keep him."

"Hit her!" Charlotte jumped up and held her fists in the air.

"As a matter of fact, I'm the sister to your husband's lover. The police found her dead in his apartment," I shot back, waiting to see her reaction. "Did he tell you all that in his so-called confession to you?"

I was on fire mad. So mad, I cursed, which I usually never did. Not only did I blush on my way back to retrieve my clothes, but I was sure I'd made the devil blush. I wasn't going to stay there a second longer.

"You didn't get any answers." Charlotte spat, "Some Betweener you are!"

"I can't take it. It makes me so mad that Sammy and Mary Katherine Hardgrove can have whatever it is they want because they have money." I jerked my sweatshirt over my head and pulled my hair out. "What were you thinking getting involved with him?"

I didn't wait for her to respond before I got the rest of my clothes on and shot out the door.

"E-scuse me!" the man called from the front porch. He waved something in the air. "You forgot to pay!"

I stalked back up to the little house and grabbed the bill.

"Four hundred dollars? For what?" My jaw dropped and my voice escalated.

"Honey, the seaweed is only the top quality. Stevon should've told you that during the consult." He put his hand on his hip and cocked his skinny panted leg out to the side. He stuck his hand out. "Cash for new clients."

"Here is what I think about your seaweed!" I held the receipt up in front of him and ripped it in half.

"Oh!" He threw his hand to his chest and his mouth flung open wide. "I never!"

"Wait!" Mary Katherine stood in the doorway of Stevon's. "I'll pay for my new friend."

She stepped out of the door and flung her wrist for the man to disappear back into the spa.

"Did you say dead?" Mary Katherine glanced at me sideways.

"I did." I jerked a piece of seaweed that was dangling from my bangs. "You paying my bill is unnecessary."

"It's the least I can do for your grief." She drummed her fingers together before she pointed behind me. "Is she . . ." Her eyes wandered to the back of the hearse.

"Do you honestly think that I'm hauling my sister around with me?" I asked.

She lifted her chin and looked down her nose at me before she tugged on the edges of the robe, gathering it together.

"You think Sammy killed her, don't you?" Mary Katherine didn't have a very good poker face. Nervously she rolled her bottom lip back and forth between her teeth.

I wasn't thinking it. I knew it and I couldn't discount Mary Katherine's hand in it, though she did seem surprised by the news. I waited to answer her. Her eyes lowered like she was really pondering what she asked me. Granny once told me that sometimes silence was an answer, but I also knew that on those CSI shows, they wait out the suspects.

She lifted her hands and tucked the edges of the towel tighter around her head. "Do you think that he came home to come clean because he knew they would find her at his apartment?" She gulped. Her throat moved up and down. "And the wife doesn't have to testify against the husband." Her eyes popped like a cork on a champagne bottle.

"I never thought of that," Charlotte grumbled. She sat on top of the hearse with her legs crossed and dangled over the side. Something else the living Charlotte would've never done.

"Diamonds Are a Girl's Best Friend" sang from the pocket of her robe.

"Excuse me." Mary Katherine stuck her hand in and pulled out her phone. She turned the screen toward me. "Him."

Sammy's name scrolled across her screen. She held up a finger and answered. I scratched an itch on my cheek.

"Hi, honey." Her voice escalated. "What?" She paused. "Where?" Her voice held concern. "Now?" She let out a few "mms," "okays" and "all rights" before she hung up the phone. She sucked in a deep breath, causing a piece of seaweed to fall off her face. "He needs me to call our attorney. The Lexington police have him in custody and are questioning him about her." There was a hint of disgust in her voice.

My mind reeled. Was the tone change because she was disgusted about her husband killing my sister or because of Charlotte?

"Are you going to help me?" I asked. "Because I am going after him. I'll do anything to see Sammy Hardgrove suffer."

"Give me your phone." She stuck her hand out. She had on the same ring Charlotte Rae was wearing. The Hardgroves must've gotten those in lots on wholesale.

"Why?" I asked.

"I'm going to plug in my number and send your number to my phone. I'm going to call you when I figure out what is going on." She jutted her hand forward. Her brows pointed into an upside-down V.

I took my phone out of my pocket and placed it in her hands. Her nails clicked away.

"There." She gave it back. "I'll be in touch. Do not come near our house or my husband until I give you a call or I won't cooperate."

She turned on her bare feet and started back up the walkway.

"Hey!" I called after her. "What's in it for you?"

It occurred to me that she was being way too accommodating for a woman whose husband just told her that he had cheated on her and then was confronted at her daily seaweed facial by her husband's lover's sister informing her that said lover was found dead at her husband's shack up apartment she didn't know anything about.

"What's in it for you?" My eyes narrowed when I asked her again. Something was wrong.

"Agreement!" Charlotte snapped. "Sammy was always telling me about their pre-nup agreement. She gets nothing if they just divorce. She gets it all if he cheats and she finds out."

"I can't be married to a murderer." The words dripped out of her mouth a little too enthusiastically.

"Oh shit." Charlotte sat stone-faced in the front of the hearse. "She's going to drag him through the mud and my name . . ."

Charlotte reminded me of the conversation I had overheard between her and Gina Marie.

My phone rang.

"Granny." My heart skipped a beat. It was the first time I'd talked to Granny since we'd slipped her a sleeping pill last night. "Hi, Granny."

I got into the hearse and headed back toward Sleepy Hollow.

"Hi?" Granny sniffed. She whispered, "Everyone is here dropping off all sorts of crap food. Even Bea Allen dropped off a pineapple upside-down cake." Granny huffed. "Pineapple upside-down cake. You and I both know that she uses crushed pineapples from a can. The juices are from concentrate. The nerve." Granny harrumphed. "And your parents are off on some safari in Africa. The emergency contact people they gave me won't be able to get them a message for at least three days!"

"Zula?" I heard Hettie Bell in the background. "Are you up?"

There was silence on the phone.

"Granny?" I asked, thinking she'd hung up on me.

"Shhh." She waited for a few more seconds. "The Auxiliary women are taking shifts sitting outside my bedroom door. I'm about sick of this. I think Hettie slipped me a mickey in that green drink she made me."

I'd rather Granny think it was Hettie than me. Being on the wrong side of Zula Fae Raines Payne was not fun.

"You are lucky to have such good friends," I said, knowing that Granny needed all the help in the world despite her hardheadedness. "And you have me."

"That is exactly what I wanted to hear. Now you listen to me, and you listen to me good." My

uh-oh alarm went off. Granny was up to something. And I had a feeling it was no good. She
continued in her hushed voice, "I got my pistol
from underneath my mattress and you are going
to drive me to Hardgrove's where I'm gonna put
a piece of lead right between Sammy Hardgrove's
eyes and if we're lucky, Gina Marie Hardgrove is
gonna get what's coming to her too."

"Whoa." I nearly drove the hearse over into the
ditch before I jerked it back. "Granny. You can't
go around shooting people to justify Charlotte
Rae's murder." I gripped the wheel and pushed
the pedal down. I had to get to the inn quicker
than a jackrabbit. Granny was about to go rogue.

"The shit she can't," Charlotte chirped from the
passenger side. "Get 'em, Granny!"

"You need to let Jack Henry be our advocate between the Lexington police and us. He will keep
us up-to-date on what is going on. Now, what
was it you said about Momma and Daddy and
Africa?"

"I said that they are on some safari way out in
the middle of Africa or something. Why on earth
you would want to sit on a stinking elephant and
sleep in the sand is beyond me, but regardless, the
emergency contact your mama gave me said they
won't be able to deliver the message for a couple
of days." Granny choked back what I could only

think to be a throat full of tears. "And to think their firstborn is sitting in some morgue waiting to be chopped on. My grandbaby." Granny sobbed on the other end of the phone.

"Granny, please let Hettie in the room." Suddenly it became apparent that Granny was losing her ever-loving mind. I understood. I was sure that if I didn't have my gift of being with Charlotte Rae, I'd be going nuts too. My caller ID clicked in. It was Jack Henry. "Granny, I've got to go. Jack Henry is calling and I want to see if he knows something about Charlotte."

"You call me back as soon as you get off with him. You understand?" Granny warned more than questioned. "Then I want you to find out when we can get Charlotte's body home."

"Yes, Granny." I clicked over. "Hello?"

"Well, Sammy Hardgrove has an alibi." Jack sounded exhausted. "He and his wife were at the airport with tickets to the Bahamas. He had an emergency at work so they didn't go."

"That's a lie!" I blurted out. "He told Mary Katherine about the affair and he came begging for forgiveness. She had no idea about the apartment."

"And Charlotte told you all this?" he asked.

"Uh-oh." Charlotte grinned. "You just got caught."

"Not exactly," I muttered under my breath. I brought the hearse to a complete stop on the side of the road. I had to get my thoughts together. The files I had taken from Hardgrove's slid off the seat and landed on the floorboard. "I . . . um . . ." I stalled for time, but then decided to just say it real fast. Like ripping off a Band-Aid. I knew it was going to hurt, but only sting for a minute. "I tracked Mary Katherine down to Stevon's on Rose in Lexington. Charlotte told me that Mary went there every morning for her seaweed facial. Did you know that a seaweed facial is like four hundred dollars?" I asked and scratched the itch on my forehead.

"And you thought it was a good idea to question her about her husband having an affair with your sister who was found dead in his apartment. Now he has an alibi with that wife." Jack's voice was flat. Not happy.

"When you put it that way." I bit my lip. My brows furrowed. "I'm just trying to help my sister." I pulled out the emotional card just in case Jack had any sympathy left for me.

"Emma Lee, you know me better than that. I thought you might be at home or with Zula grieving, not traipsing off for a facial to pump someone for information. Besides, don't you think the homicide department in Lexington has followed up on all these leads?"

"Homicide?" I asked.

"They have officially named Charlotte a murder victim." His words stung now that her death had been confirmed a homicide, even though I already knew it.

"I wasn't traipsing." I hated that word. "I was investigating my Betweener client's leads. I still have a job to do even if it is my sister."

"Your job is to stay out of it." Jack's voice was stern, yet it was comforting to know he cared as much as he did. "Besides, my buddy at the police department told me that they have all the sufficient evidence that clears Sammy and Mary Katherine Hardgrove."

"Like what?" The bitter, scorned wife's knowledge of the affair was definitely a good reason for Mary to go crazy and I was sure she killed Charlotte. It was the only thing that made sense. Of course Charlotte could be snarky, but everyone still liked her. Everyone but a betrayed wife.

"They pulled their plane tickets, they even pulled the security footage at the Bluegrass Airport. Sure enough, Sammy and Mary Katherine were having a fight right before the security entrance around the same time the coroner said Charlotte Rae was killed. Oh my God," Jack gasped.

"What?"

"You need to hurry back." His voice was tight. "Zula Fae is standing in the middle of the gazebo with that megaphone of hers. Her hair is sticking up all over her head and she's got on a white nightdress with those leather motorcycle boots she likes to wear."

Taking a deep breath, I said, "Oh, Jack. I think Granny has gone nuts."

I pushed the End button, immediately dialed Doc Clyde, and hit the gas pedal. I've had his number on speed dial since I'd been diagnosed with the "Funeral Trauma."

Ina Claire Nell answered the phone. "Doc Clyde's office. How can I help you?"

"Ina Claire, it's Emma Lee. Can I talk to Doc?" I questioned in a rush. The tree lines on the side of the road were just one long line of green as the hearse zoomed down the country roads leading me back to Sleepy Hollow.

"Hmm. Let me guess, you are seeing the ghost of Sissy Phillips?" Her voice was cloaked in thick sarcasm.

"Look out your window," I said with knots in my stomach. "It's not me. It's Granny."

The squeak of a chair and the groan of exasperation came through the phone. I could picture her now getting up from behind her desk and nervously fidgeting with her blond hair she kept in an updo. When the door hinges creaked, I could visualize her walking from the patient hallway into the waiting room. With my ear pressed tight to the phone, I waited to hear her reaction.

"Ohhhh." The gasp on the other end of the phone made my inner *God, help me* meter go off. Granny was worse than Jack had told me or that I'd imagined. Ina never got back on the phone. It seemed she laid it down and got so distracted by Granny that she forgot I was on there, which made me drive even faster.

There was a crowd gathered in the town square. Jack Henry, Hettie Bell and Mable Claire were all running after Granny. Granny looked like a ball of fire as she darted in and out of the crowd with the megaphone to her mouth.

I didn't bother trying to park the hearse in Eternal Slumber's driveway. The hearse came to an abrupt stop when it hit the curb. I flung the gear shift in Park and jumped out, leaving the door hanging open.

"One million dollars!" There wasn't nothing wrong with Granny's balance or reflexes. She darted between everyone's arms, held the megaphone up to her mouth with one hand and waved some papers in the air with the other. "The inn is your reward if you have the clue or answers to who killed my granddaughter, Charlotte Rae Raines! Someone has information. No questions asked. The inn deed will be signed over to you!"

"Granny!" I screamed, flailed my arms and bounced on the balls of my feet. I tried to be polite and smile at all of our neighbors, but it was just too hard to keep the good southern girl composure Granny had always boasted about when she couldn't do it herself. "Granny!" I screamed louder.

"Oh my God," Jack Henry groaned and ran his hands through his hair before he darted around to grab Granny.

"Granny!" I screamed so loud I got dizzy.

She stopped. Mable Claire tackled Granny. Coins from her pockets went flying everywhere and the kids in the crowd scattered, picking up the pennies and dimes before running off.

"There will be no one million dollars." Jack Henry tried to hush the crowd.

"Oh yes there is!" Granny could still scream with Mable sitting on top of her. Her legs reminded me of the wicked witch when the house fell on top of her. "I dee-clare, Mable, if you don't get off of me I will knock you into next year when you do get up off me!" Granny shook her body. Mable Claire hung on for dear life.

"Granny." I bent over with my hands on my knees, gasping for air. "Get a hold of yourself."

A little sprig of red hair was all you could see under Mable Claire's body. Jack Henry looked at me and my temples began to throb.

"Me?" Granny bellowed. "You are the one with the 'Funeral Trauma.'" She grunted and finally stopped wiggling around.

"This is not helping anyone." I cursed under a deep breath and scratched my neck. Scratching felt so good, I almost acted like a dog and thumped my foot on the ground.

"And do you know how many phone calls I'm going to get with leads that are going to go nowhere because you've offered the one million dollars?" Jack Henry huffed.

"This is why you need to do yoga." Hettie Bell planted her hands on her hips and pointed between me and Granny. "For mental and physical health."

"Oh my goodness," Charlotte chirped from behind me. "Help her up."

"Come on, Mable." I grabbed her by the arm and helped her to her feet. She tugged the hem of her house dress down.

"Granny?" I grimaced when she didn't move. She was breathing and I was sure she was assessing what had just taken place in front of all of Sleepy Hollow. Granny was a good southern woman who loved a good crazy situation but not when it involved our family, much less her.

She turned her face up to me. Something flickered in her eyes. Her mouth opened. She hooted, she snorted, she sniggered.

"I'm gonna find out who killed my granddaughter," Granny slurred, grinned and fell back down on her face.

I waved my hand in front of my face. The stink was thick and heavy like a good bourbon. "Has Granny been drinking?" I looked up at Hettie, who was supposed to be watching Granny.

"I don't know what she was doing in that room." Hettie's brows dipped in a frown. "I did exactly what the Auxiliary women told me to do." We stood over Granny in awe. I'd never seen her drink anything heavier than her own sweet tea. "They told me to check on her a few times an hour. Let her come and go as she pleased."

"And make sure she eats," Mable Claire chimed in and adjusted her glasses up on her nose and planted her stout body next to Granny's lifeless one.

"It looks like the entire Raines regime has all gone nuts." Bea Allen Burns sashayed up and glanced down at Granny, then slid her eyes to me.

"Oh hush," I warned her.

Granny jumped up, looking like a madwoman, cursing so much I'm sure the devil was blushing. She danced around Mable Claire with both fists in the air. "I told you that I was gonna git you." Granny took a jab as Mable Claire ducked behind me. Jack rushed over and grabbed Granny, locking her in his arms. It didn't stop her. She stomped her feet, landing them like heavy weights on Jack's feet. He grimaced.

"Emma Lee, get a hold of your granny!" Mable Claire squealed.

"I'm sorry," I mouthed to Jack Henry for not only Granny's behavior but the thought of all these people trying to find leads on Charlotte's death and calling in with dead ends that he was going to have to spend most of his time following up on.

"First, the prodigal granddaughter leaves the family for a competing funeral home, has an affair with the owner, and then gets murdered. Then there is you." Bea Allen pointed her long bony finger at me and took a long look-see at Granny stuffed in Jack's arms. Her accusing eyes looked up at me, her mouth spread into a thin-lipped smile. "Everyone, Burns Funeral is having a half-off sale for all pre-need arrangements for a limited time. I hope y'all take time to talk to all your friends and loved ones about their eternal resting place and come to Burns."

A low murmur spread over the crowd.

"One million dollars and now half off funeral arrangements?" Fluggie Callahan, editor-in-chief of the *Sleepy Hollow Gazette* scribbled away on her notepad. "I'd like to print your sale." She looked at Bea Allen.

I glared and thought very bad thoughts that made me think I should go see Pastor Brown. Her bony finger lifted to her ear and she did crazy circles around it.

"That's enough, Ms. Burns." Jack stepped up. He lifted his hands in the air. "Everyone can go home now. There is nothing here to see but a grieving family. I'm sure we have all had a moment like this."

"Does that mean the million-dollar reward is no longer on the table?" John Howard, of all people, spoke up over the crowd. He stood in the back with Arley Burgin. After I gave him the death stare, he tapped Arley on the arm and they walked across the town square to Eternal Slumber. Jack Henry had Granny by the arms, guiding her the opposite direction to the inn.

"Don't worry about Zula." Hettie shot me a twisted smile.

"Oh, because you are looking after her so good?" I retorted tartly.

"Emma Lee, I'm doing the best I can. You are her granddaughter, the sister of Charlotte. Why aren't you looking after her?" Hettie's tone had turned chilly.

"I'm trying to figure out what happened to Charlotte. Plus, I had to go identify her and do all the things I need to do to get her body here." Tears puddled in my eyes.

"How insensitive of me." Hettie hugged me. "I'm so sorry. I know you and Charlotte didn't see eye to eye, but she's still your sister."

"Who does she think she is?" Charlotte snarled. "She just thought she'd waltz right into town and steal our grandmother from us?"

"You have really helped out over the past couple of years. Granny thinks of you as much of a granddaughter as she does me and Charlotte." I wanted Hettie to know how much I appreciated her and let Charlotte know how much Hettie had helped out, especially since Charlotte quit her job at Eternal Slumber and went to Hardgrove's.

From a distance I watched Charlotte skitter up next to Granny as she and Jack Henry disappeared into the door of the inn.

Chapter 11

After the stunt Granny had pulled, I had a massive headache. I let Jack Henry get Granny settled at the inn to sleep off her drunken stupor while I went back to take a nap.

The knock at the door woke me up. I rolled to my side and looked at the clock. The ghost cat was snugged into a tiny ball on a pillow. It was seven o'clock at night and I had slept the day away. Stress did funny things to people and I was still exhausted. Mentally.

The knock got louder.

"Hey." Jack Henry stood on the other side. The warmth in his smile was in the tone of his voice. "I let you have some space today. I figured you needed it, so I brought you dinner." He held up a familiar brown sack.

"Chinese." A happy sigh escaped my lips and my stomach growled. I stepped back and held the door open. "Get in here."

"You go sit in the family room and I'll go grab some paper plates from the kitchen." Jack's voice was stern. On his way down the hall, he called over my shoulder, "You wouldn't believe how many calls I've had about leads and the one-million-dollar reward."

I flipped the light on and sat on the couch, putting the sack on the coffee table. My mouth watered from the smell of the Chinese food. I pushed my bangs out of the way, giving my forehead a good scratch. I was beginning to wonder if I might be allergic to the cat, even though it'd been around a few days.

"I even got a call about some evidence in a pumpkin patch in the country." He laughed, walking back in with a couple paper plates and two wineglasses.

"I can only imagine the calls." I laughed, thinking about Jack tromping through a pumpkin patch.

I smiled up at him. His brows furrowed and his hands dropped with the plates and glasses by his side.

"What?" I asked.

"What happened to your face?" He bent down between my legs and took a good look. I put my hands on my face. "You have some sort of rash."

I sprang up and ran into the hall to look in the mirror over the hallway table. The small dots trailed along my forehead, down my temple and across my chin. I rubbed my hand over my face as though I was going to rub it away.

"What are you doing?" I asked Jack who was standing behind me on his cell phone.

"I'm calling Doc Clyde."

"I'm sure it's stress." I leaned closer to the mirror and continued to rub, saying to myself because Jack walked down the hall to talk, "Or the cat."

"He said he's on his way." Jack held my chin in his fingers and tilted my head closer to the light to get a better look. Carefully and softly, he ran the pad of his finger along the rash. A cute puppy dog look on his face melted my heart. "Does it itch?"

"I was itching earlier in the hearse." I remembered talking to Charlotte and having an itch.

I walked into the family room and opened the sack. I took out an egg roll and chomped down on it. With a mouthful of shredded cabbage and fried dough, I said, "It was probably that damn seaweed."

Jack clapped his hands and I nearly dropped my precious egg roll.

"I bet you are right." He rushed to the door when someone knocked on it. "Come on in," I heard Jack say, inviting Doc into the apartment. "She's in there."

"Hey, Doc." I waved what little bit of egg roll was left in front of me. "This rash hasn't stopped my appetite."

He walked over and put his little doctor bag down next to the Chinese food.

"Hmm." He tilted his head and used an otoscope light to look at my face. He wasn't nearly as gentle as Jack. "Yep, definitely a rash."

"Tell me something she doesn't already know." Sarcasm dripped out of Charlotte's mouth. I jerked my head toward her wondering where she'd been all this time. "He's been with Granny all day. Gave her some sedatives and knocked her out."

"I'm sorry about Charlotte." Doc pulled the otoscope down and looked at me. "It's such a shock. I gave Zula some sedatives to keep her calm. From what I understand she doesn't want to have the funeral until your parents get here and that could take a week."

"Thank you." I smiled. "I think I got the rash from a seaweed facial I had this morning."

"This is definitely not a stress rash based on the raised bumps and abrasions." He put the scope away and took a pad and pen out of his bag. "I'm going to prescribe a low dose steroid cream." He scribbled away. "I'm going to go back and sit with Zula. If you have any issues, just pop over there to see me or call Ina Claire for an appointment."

"Thanks, Doc." Jack Henry shook the doctor's hand and led him out into the hallway.

"I want you to watch her for the 'Funeral Trauma.' This type of death could really do a number on her mentally," Doc Clyde whispered.

"I'll be sure to do that," Jack Henry assured him and the door closed. "So she's here?"

"Yep." I pointed over by the television and took the Chinese food boxes out of the bag before distributing some on our plates. "I'll have a big ole glass of wine."

Jack uncorked the wine and poured two very generous glassfuls.

"Unfortunately, the one thing that did pan out today was Sammy and his wife are not suspects. Apparently he was supposed to meet up with Charlotte on the vacation, and when Mary Katherine got the Visa bill, she noticed the airline's charge on it and called the airlines only to find out his plane didn't go anywhere near Des Moines like Sammy had told her. You could only imagine his surprise when he was through security and she was sitting at the gate with her carry-on in her grip." Jack looked over at the space where I had pointed and where Charlotte was. "He said that he didn't know why Charlotte was at the apartment."

Jack made a very good point. I looked at Charlotte and she shrugged at me. I shook my head at Jack.

"I'm telling you, there is footage of him at the airport with Mary Katherine in what looks to be a very heated discussion around Charlotte's time of death."

"And that seals the deal." I didn't bother using the chopsticks. I was starving and needed to shovel it in. I took a forkful of moo-goo and pushed it in my mouth. "I guess we are going to have to go through all the files."

"What files?" Jack Henry questioned.

"I, um, kinda stole the files from Charlotte's office the day I trespassed." I knew this wasn't going to sit well with him. And after he downed the glass of wine and refilled it, I was right.

"Emma." He sighed. "I told you that you have to let the police handle this. They need those files. And if I tell them you took them, you will go to jail. That would be no help to your sister at all."

"So, what do you expect me to do?" I asked and drank the rest of my glass. "I guess I could give them back to Arley."

"Arley? The grave digger at Hardgrove's and

the guy on the Eternal Slumber softball team?"
He threw his head back with an exasperated gasp.
"This is getting worse and worse."

"Oops." I bit my lip. "I didn't tell you that part?"
I tried to play stupid but he knew better. I was
far from dumb and everything I did was always
deliberate.

"I don't want to know any more. You just give
him back those files and get him to put them back
where you found them and hope he keeps his
mouth closed about you stealing them."

Chapter 12

The next morning, I knew I had to get up and get the files back to Hardgrove's before anyone saw me. The cop told Arley Burgin to keep me off the property and I was sure the cop told everyone else who worked there that too. Plus, I didn't know exactly how I was going to get in there.

"You could wear a costume," Charlotte chimed in over the sound of the shower.

Ghost Charlotte had lost her ever-lovin' mind. "Do ghosts lose all track of time, because it's clearly not Halloween."

I peeled back the curtain and Charlotte was sitting on the toilet with her legs crossed, swinging the top one to and fro. "I know you can't go in as Emma Lee."

I shut the curtain back and scrubbed the shampoo in my hair. The foam was thick. With my eyes closed, I stood under the showerhead and let the water run over me, wishing it were ideas instead of water.

My eyes popped open and I turned the water off. The curtain rings screeched along the shower rod when I flung the curtain open. "I've got an idea!"

"Oh no. I don't like the excitement in your voice." Charlotte watched me jump out of the shower and grab the towel from the towel rack on my way out.

I put the towel around me and tucked the edge in and hurried down the hall and into the funeral home.

"What?" Charlotte asked, following me down the long hall.

"You know how we have clients bring in clothes for Mary Anna to dress their loved ones?" I opened my office door and headed straight to the office walk-in closet where I kept my funeral clothes and other items the clients' families hadn't picked up. Things like extra clothes. "Where is it?" I pushed the hangers with the bags attached to them. The bags held the extra clothes clients would bring for their loved ones.

I always asked my clients to bring a couple outfits just in case the one outfit they picked out for their loved one to be buried in just didn't fit right.

In mortuary school, there was an entire class on how to dress a corpse. It was more involved than just sticking a shirt and tie on them. Corpses become stiff and it was easier to cut the shirts or jackets in half up the back and dress each side, tucking in the back edges.

"Voila!" I grabbed the hanger I knew was my ticket into Hardgrove's.

"Beatrice Roan?" Charlotte looked at the tag. "She's been dead for years." Charlotte looked off into the distance. She smiled. "She sure was a lot of fun."

"She was." I sucked in a deep breath. "Do you remember why she was so much fun?"

"Duh." Charlotte stuck her hands on her hips. "Because she always"—her eyes grew big and so did her grin—"always dressed up in Halloween costumes even though it wasn't Halloween!" She clapped her hands in delight.

"And her family brought both of Beatrice's nun outfits." I wiggled my brows and held the hanger with the bag up between our faces. "And I only used one. And this is the one they left behind."

"That's right." Charlotte snapped her fingers. "I remember I tried to talk them out of burying her in the nun costume, but they insisted that she be buried in one of the nun costumes and with the Baptist hymnal so she was guaranteed to get into heaven."

"Right as rain." I took the bag off the hook of the hanger and took out the extra nun outfit. "It's perfect."

"Well, you better get back in there and get it on." She pointed to the door of the office. "But what about the hearse? Everyone knows you drive that hearse."

"Oh." My ride was something I hadn't thought of. "Thank God you are a ghost and can meet me places."

"I don't like the sound of that," Charlotte said.

"Trust me." I couldn't help but think I was a genius. "Just meet me at Hardgrove's in forty-five minutes."

It didn't take long for me to get ready. I didn't bother putting on makeup or fixing my hair. There was no need if I was going to be tucking it under the bandeau. I used a belt underneath the habit and strapped the files there so they couldn't be seen. With Granny knocked out, I snuck into the kitchen door of the inn and grabbed her moped keys off the hook by the door. After I unchained the moped from around the big oak tree in the front of the inn, I pulled the throttle down as far as it would go. With the wind blowing the veil behind me, I held on tight and let the moped whiz under me all the way to Lexington.

Arley stood on the sidewalk of Hardgrove's

with a shovel in his hands and the darn security guard was next to him. They looked at me when I pulled up. My stomach churned. I hoped and prayed they didn't recognize me.

"Good day." I slightly nodded, avoiding eye contact. For some unknown reason, a British accent came out of me. "Haven't you seen a sister drive a moped?"

"No, sister, but you sure do look funny." Arley snickered. The guard used the back of his hand to smack Arley on the arm.

"I'm sorry, sister." The guard apologized to me. "My friend here doesn't go to Catholic church."

"It's okay, son." I did a quick sign of the cross and scurried into Hardgrove's. I looked up to the sky and whispered, "Please, forgive me."

"He will if you find out who murdered me." Charlotte had ghosted herself into the lobby of Hardgrove's.

"Sister?" The assistant stood up out of respect. I felt a little bad, but not bad enough since she was so nasty the other morning. "Can I help you?"

"I . . ." I swallowed. I never imagined she'd be here this early.

"Tell her you are here to bless the chapel." Charlotte casually leaned up against the desk and drummed her fingers on top of it.

"I'm here to bless the chapel." I smiled and

looked down, moving my mouth as if I was saying a silent prayer. "For the wedding of Candy."

"No." Charlotte groaned.

"That wedding has been canceled." The receptionist looked at me.

"Yes. I'm cleansing the bad vibes." I did a sign of the cross toward her.

"You are going to hell." Charlotte laughed. "And I love it."

"Oh." The receptionist gulped. "You can go on back."

"Thank you, dearie." The British accent was coming out with ease.

"And why are you acting like a nun from England?" Charlotte led the way to her office.

When we were safely inside, I pulled the files from underneath the habit and Candy's file was on top.

"Why on earth would Candy cancel her wedding?" I asked. "They were all set to go."

"Her and her mama were so mad about the flowers." Charlotte laughed. "I know that I really did try to sell you and Granny on the idea of the Legacy Center and all the things we do here, but the truth is, people like Candy's family, they just have a hard time wrapping their heads around walking down the aisle to begin a new life while another family is in the next room saying goodbye to a life."

"That is exactly what I said." I opened the file

cabinet and started to put the files back in just like Jack Henry had told me. "But I just can't stop thinking about them the day Granny and I was here." I shook my head. "Princess Candy with the two-toned hair and the scrawny boy?" I asked, vividly remembering the joy I took out of hearing the accusations fly at Charlotte when the mom went cuckoo on her.

"Yeah. Well, they did threaten me." Charlotte's voice drifted off. She looked out the window for a second. "I did go to their house, but I can't remember what happened."

"Did you go alone?" I asked.

"No." Her eyes popped open. "Sammy and I were out to dinner and Melinda, the mama, was there. I got a call from her saying that she knew I was sleeping with Sammy and she knew Mary Katherine from school and she was going to tell her if I didn't . . ." Charlotte tapped her temple.

"Didn't what?" I encouraged her to hurry up.

"Shoot." Her chin dropped. Her lips turned down. "I can't remember now."

"Well then." I shut the file drawer but kept out Candy's file and lifted up the habit and strapped the file back under the belt. "We are going to go pay her a visit."

"Like that?" Charlotte's eyes drew up and down my outfit.

"It's been good so far." I winked and waved. "I'll see you there."

"Sister?" Arley stood at the door just as I was walking toward it. "Are you lost?"

"Oh no." I lifted my hands and chin in the air. The British accent automatically came back. "I was sent here by a higher power to bless this room for some reason."

I brought my hands together in front of me and whispered gibberish under my breath. Slightly I squinted toward Arley and he had pulled his hat off his head and lowered it as if he were praying.

"I'll be on my way now, son." I swept past him and made sure I didn't give him eye contact.

"Sister." Arley's voice made my skin crawl when he called me back. The worst situation I could imagine. "I, umm." He paused. I stopped with my back to him. "I need to confess something."

I twirled around.

"Something about why I was summoned by the Great One?" I refused to say God because I was lying. Did he know something? I looked at Charlotte's name plate to make it seem like I had no idea whose office it was, "Charlotte Raines?"

Slowly he nodded his head.

"Go on, my son." I tilted my chin slightly down and to the side, keeping my eyes lowered the whole time.

"I think she came across a crime that is being committed here in the Legacy Center and that's why someone killed her." His voice cracked.

"A crime? Ahem," I cleared my voice when I realized my British accent left me. "A crime was committed here with Charlotte Raines?"

"Yes, ma'am. Sister," he corrected himself. "She's dead."

At the same time, I drew in a deep gasp and planted my hand on my chest.

"Dear son, do you need to tell me something?" I asked. "In strict confidence, of course."

Strict confidence, my ass. I glared at him and thought evil thoughts.

"I heard that Ms. Charlotte had made some people mad."

"Mad? Like who?" I asked trying to get more out of him, but not alarm him.

"I don't know. I'm feeling guilty because I probably should've said something but I didn't and now she's dead." Arley hung his head. His hair flung down in his face. His hands were folded in front of him.

"Who did you hear this from?" I asked.

"Aren't you going to tell me that I'm forgiven?" Arley's voice bit back.

"You will be forgiven after you give me a reason to forgive you, like"—I rolled my wrist in front of him to encourage him to come forth with what he knew—"give me the name who you heard this from."

"I don't know." Arley sulked. "I just know that she made some pregnant girl and her mama mad. I even heard them threaten Ms. Raines."

"You are forgiven," I said, realizing he had no idea what Charlotte had run up on, but placed Candy at the scene. I wasn't sure if Charlotte knew what she had seen because she never mentioned running into something bad. I started to walk toward the front of the building.

"Wait," Arley called out from behind. "Aren't you going to do that cross thing so I can be forgiven?"

Arley Burgin was beginning to get on my nerves. Harmless, but on my nerves. I didn't have time for this. I had to get to Candy's and figure out what her crazy mama knew about the affair.

"Yeah, yeah." I turned around. Walking backward I did the sign of the cross in the air before I twirled back around and headed straight out the door, and zoomed down the driveway of Hardgrove's.

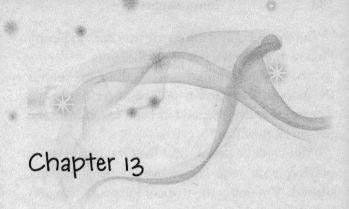

Chapter 13

The more I tried to reason in my head that Sammy Hardgrove had killed Charlotte, the less he became my number one suspect. His sister, Gina Marie, was an altogether different story.

She was the one who stood to gain the most from Charlotte's death. If Charlotte was out of the way, maybe Sammy and Mary Katherine would reconcile and Mary Katherine would not get some of the business like Gina Marie had said in her heated discussion with Charlotte.

Obviously, Melinda and Candy were suspects since there were two people who had heard them threaten Charlotte—me and Arley. I was going to have to go see all three of them.

The sirens behind me on my way back to Sleepy Hollow brought me out of my thoughts.

"Sister." The familiar voice walked up behind the moped. "I'm sorry to pull you over, but I have a report that this moped has been stolen from the Sleepy Hollow Inn."

"You can't be serious?" I kept my head down, playing with Jack Henry. My British voice returned. "I'm doing the work of the good man and you think that I stole a moped?"

"Sister, I'm sorry and I do feel bad for pulling you over, but I will need to see some sort of proof that you own this moped." Jack was so cute in his politeness, I figured I could toy with him a bit.

"What if I take you back over behind those woods and give you a romp you will never forget? I have so much pent-up passion under this robe that it's time I release the inner goddess in me." I let out a little giggle.

"Um . . ." Jack stuttered, "Sister, I don't think that's appropriate."

"Oh, it's so appropriate." I lifted my hands in the air and stared at him, using my real voice. "Come here, big boy."

Jack's mouth dropped and his eyes nearly bugged out of his head. "Emma Lee Raines, what the hell are you doing?"

I gulped. "I thought you might think this was funny."

When Jack Henry cursed, I knew he wasn't happy.

"A nun is not funny. A nun on a stolen moped is definitely not funny. A nun with a supercharged dirty mind . . ." He didn't finish his sentence; he simply shook his head. A slow smile crept up on his lips, making my toes curl.

"I might be dressed as a nun, but my thoughts are not pure." I winked.

"Emma." He blushed. "I kinda like it, but you took the moped?"

"Yes." I bit my lip, squinted my nose, and closed my eyes. I knew what was coming next.

"And why are you dressed as a nun?" he asked.

"Long story over coffee?" I asked and scratched my chin. "I need to get this thing off, get to the pharmacy to pick up my prescription for this darn rash, and I need a coffee."

"Fine. But you explain to Zula why you took her moped. She freaked out." He sucked in a deep breath before he bent down to kiss me, but he pulled away. "Something just isn't right kissing a nun."

"Give me a kiss." I grabbed his uniform shirt and twisted it in my fist, bringing him closer.

I slapped a big sloppy kiss on him just as a car passed and honked at us. "I'll see you at Higher Grounds in a half hour." I winked, waved and zoomed off, leaving him in the dust.

The news crew was knocking on the door of the Sleepy Hollow Inn when I got back into town and chained up the moped on the oak. Before they could run down the front steps of the inn and get me on camera, I ran to the back of the inn and rushed in the kitchen door.

"Is the good Lord coming to get me?" Granny held her heart and jumped back into the kitchen table chair.

"What?" I asked.

"Emma?" Granny put her hand on the table and eased up to standing. "Well, clutch my pearls, what on God's green earth are you doing in that outfit? Please, tell me you haven't had a case of the 'Funeral Trauma' and gone to join the Catholic Church. We are Baptist, baby. Southern Baptist," Granny cried. "Both of us can't be crazy. Who will run Eternal Slumber with me and you in the nut-house and Charlotte six feet under?"

"No." I ripped the bandeau off my head. "I had to go incognito and use your scooter because everyone is all hovering over me because of Charlotte." I bent my head down and pretended to say a silent prayer in honor of Charlotte and for good measure with Granny. "I'm trying to hurry this investigation along and figure out who hurt Charlotte."

"I heard Doc Clyde came over last night." Granny eased back down in the chair.

"News travels fast." I groaned and noticed how disheveled Granny looked. Her normally vibrant short red hair was matted down on the side and the back while the other side was sticking straight out. I sat down in the chair next to her and scooted it closer. "Granny, are you going to be okay?"

"I feel like the wind has been knocked out of my sail." The corners of Granny's lips dipped down. "It ain't natural for your grandchildren to pass before you do. And Charlotte Rae had some flaws, but not enough for someone to kill her."

"I do not have flaws." Charlotte appeared and huffed over to the stove. "Emma." She pointed down into Granny's teapot on the stove.

I got up and looked at it. The water had boiled and the tea bags were practically dried and the burner was still on low.

"Granny!" I grabbed the steel handle and nearly burned my hand off. "You can't be making tea right now. Where is Hettie?"

"Hettie had to do yoga and she sent Beulah

Paige." Granny jerked her head toward the swinging door between the kitchen and the rest of the inn.

I hit the swinging door and walked down the hall looking for Beulah Paige Bellefry. The loud snoring led me straight to the front sitting room where Beulah was laid out on the sofa in her perfect, coifed style. She had on a pantsuit, her pearls strapped around her neck and wrists and not a single hair out of place.

"Beulah!" I screamed, making her jump to her feet.

"Emma Lee Raines, you are crazy!" She brushed her hands down her suit jacket. "Heavens to Betsy, I hope Doc Clyde gave you some good medication last night because if you haven't noticed, you have on a nun's outfit."

"So you are the one spreading the rumors about Doc Clyde coming over." I glared at her.

"What do you want?" she asked in her long southern drawl.

"You aren't taking care of Granny," I stated. "She's about to burn the kitchen down."

"She was passed out cold when I got here." Beulah shoved past me and down the hall into the kitchen. I followed her. "Zula Fae Raines Payne, you get back up in that bed."

"Have you lost your ever-loving mind?"

Granny asked. "I'll do no such thing. I'm gonna find out who did this to my granddaughter." Granny glanced up at the clock. "That darn news should be here anytime."

"News?" I asked, not telling her that they were outside when I had gotten there.

"I'm going to sell this place and give the one-million-dollar reward." Granny wrung her hands and got back up from the chair. She skedaddled over to the teapot, filling it back up and sticking in more tea bags. "They are going to love my tea."

Instantly my mouth watered. Granny was right. They would love her iced tea. She made the best tea in the entire state of Kentucky.

"There is no such thing going to happen." I nixed any notions Granny had in that little red head of hers. "Besides, you can't be on camera looking like that."

"I look bad?" Her hand felt around her head and she dipped down, looking at her reflection in the oven door. "I'll be. I look like the last rose of summer.

"I still haven't heard from your parents," she called before she scurried out of the kitchen. When I felt like she had climbed the steps to her bedroom, I turned to Beulah as I heard Granny say, "I still haven't heard when we are getting Charlotte's body back."

"You listen to me." I stalked closer to Beulah. "You better take good care of her before I get back. And don't you let her talk to any news media. You hear me?"

"Yes, sister." Beulah gave me the stink eye before she pushed me out of her way and walked over to the boiling tea water, stirring it slowly.

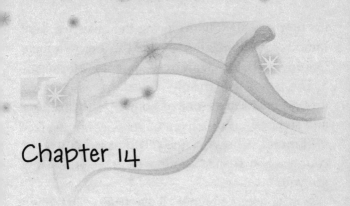

Chapter 14

Charlotte had conveniently disappeared again while I rushed home and changed my clothes before I headed down to Higher Grounds. I had tucked Candy's file in the bedroom dresser drawer. Charlotte needed to tell me what she remembered about Melinda and her veiled threats.

It was a nice day so I decided to walk down to the café. The fresh air would do me good and help clear out some of the jumble up there.

Higher Grounds was located on the Main Street right in front of the town square. The sun was already peering down and illuminating the beautiful park in the middle of Sleepy Hollow. The backdrop of the mountains was breathtaking. And to think that there were hikers and climbers up there already exploring the caves we were famous for. I'd imagine some of the inn customers Granny had kicked out were up there camping.

The smell of freshly baked bread twirled around my head as soon as I opened the café door and stepped inside.

"Emma!" Cheryl Lynne yelled from behind the counter. She rushed around to greet me. "How are you?"

"Oh, you know. Numb." It was true. Even though I was acting like a madwoman trying to figure out who killed Charlotte. I still had those moments where I couldn't believe that after I did figure out who killed her, that I truly wouldn't see her again. Thinking about it brought tears to my eyes.

"Oh, honey." Cheryl put her arms around me and pulled me in for a big hug.

Out of nowhere, the waterworks were turned on and I sobbed for the very first time about Charlotte. Cheryl gently patted my back.

I pulled away and took the paper napkin she handed me and wiped my face off.

"And I thought I was doing good," I said.

"Clearly you aren't and that rash on your face is stress." She nodded her head. "You need a good cup of coffee." She held up her finger and hurried back around the counter. "And a muffin."

"Make it two." I pointed to the two-person café

table next to the window. "Jack Henry is going to meet me in a minute."

"You got it." Cheryl went to work on my order while I took my seat at the table.

"Sorry I'm late." Jack kissed the top of my head and took the seat across from me.

"No problem." I smiled at my handsome boyfriend, grateful he was here.

"Here you go." Cheryl put a plate with two big chocolate chip muffins on it in the middle of the round, glass-top table and came back with two cups of coffee and a carafe. "You two take all the time you need. Emma, I've got a box of pastries and pimento cheese finger sandwiches for you to take home with you."

"Thank you." I was thankful for the small town we lived in. When I had gone back to change my clothes, Vernon Baxter had left a note on my apartment door. He wrote that there was plenty of food in the kitchen from people hearing about Charlotte. Food was comfort in the south and there was no time like a funeral to need comfort.

"What was up with the nun thing?" Jack asked with a mouthful of muffin.

"You told me to get the files back into Hardgrove's." I smiled. "I couldn't just waltz in there, so I used Beatrice Roan's nun costume her family had left as a backup outfit for her funeral.

They never picked it up and I had it in the office closet."

"Pretty smart if it worked." Jack picked up the coffee and took a drink. "Dangerous, but smart."

"I couldn't drive the hearse, so I used Granny's moped thinking she wouldn't notice since Doc Clyde had given her those sleeping pills. I was wrong. Plus she's still hell-bent on doing the one-million-dollar reward." This was when I hated being a Betweener and keeping it from Granny. "I wish I could tell her Charlotte is here."

"Maybe you can." Charlotte sat cross-legged in the window. Her eyes closed as the warmth of the sun beamed down on her.

"How?" I asked with sarcasm.

"How what?" Jack asked, looking at me strangely.

"Charlotte." I pointed to the window. "Oops." I looked around to make sure no one was looking. It was times like this when people saw me talking into the empty space around me that made them think I had the "Funeral Trauma."

"Zula does not need to know about this Be-tweener gig." Jack knew it wasn't a good idea, just like I did. "We really need to go visit that psychic again to tell her that it's just not your clients you are seeing now."

"We do." My eyes were drawn to the outside

where the orange tabby narrowly missed getting hit by a car. I drew in a quick breath.

"What now?" Jack asked.

"The cat nearly got hit, but I'm sure it can't die twice." I shrugged and went back to my muffin.

"Nope, they have nine lives." Jack laughed at his own joke. "Apparently Cat used all his."

"Good one." I smiled at his contagious laughter and cuteness. "Anyways, I returned the files with no problem, but Arley took the opportunity to feel like he needed to confess."

"To you?"

"Duh, nun," I reminded him. "He said that he felt bad because he thinks Charlotte was threatened by a disgruntled client. When I pressed him, saying God needed his full confession, he got tight-lipped."

"Emma Lee, have you no shame?"

"Not when it comes to why my sister was killed." I looked out the café window that overlooked the town square. Cat was running up to the people and sniffing their shoes before he darted to the next. It looked like he was trying to find a scent. I looked over at Jack. I said, "Maybe you can put the squeeze on Arley at softball practice."

"He wasn't there last night." Jack popped the last bite of his muffin in his mouth. "Something about his dad being sick."

"Oh, that's right." I remembered him telling me his dad had a bad case of COPD. "He did mention his dad was on oxygen all the time."

"That's awful." Jack pushed the cup of coffee away from him. We stopped talking when Cheryl dropped off the check and put the bag of goodies for me to take on the table.

I thanked her and she mouthed, "You're welcome."

"How is your rash?" Jack looked at my chin, which was the worst part.

"Itchy. Which means I better get going. The ointment Doc prescribed is probably ready at the pharmacy." I got up and walked over to him. "I understand I've got some good food waiting back at my kitchen, so you want to come by tonight for a smorgasbord of food?"

"You bet." He stood up and gave me the "we are in public" kiss. Nothing to make my toes curl or heart flutter. "My mom even made some lasagna for you."

"Really?" I drew back. "Well, well, it took my sister's death for her to like me?"

"Didn't say she liked you." He winked and smacked my tushy.

"Officer Ross, that's off-limits while you are in that uniform." I flirted before walking out the door.

Cat saw me walk out and darted across the

street, barely being missed by another car. I was beginning to see exactly how he had died. There was no way I was going to track down an owner of a car that might've hit and killed Cat.

After grabbing the file and keys to the hearse, I was on my way and happy that Charlotte joined me.

"Did you love him?" I wondered about Charlotte and Sammy.

"*Love* is a strong word, but Sammy was kind." Charlotte gestured to the house I was looking for coming up.

It wasn't the best subdivision to live in. The ranch homes looked like small boxes. It was as though the developer took a mound of building supplies, and used the same cookie cutter, plopping the same house down every few inches. Each house had a front door and a window on each side. There was a driveway with a car port at the end and a square concrete slab under the front door, big enough for two people to stand on.

I pulled up to the house and took a look around. I wanted to get to the bottom of what happened to Charlotte, but not at my own expense.

"I know he is married and I know he was never going to leave Mary." Charlotte sighed. "That is what's so appealing. He didn't want any more than what I wanted." Charlotte looked at me. "Oh, stop getting all high and moral on me. I know it was wrong and I do have a little knot in my stomach that when I do face"—she pointed her finger up to the sky—"you know who, that He's going to ask me why I slept with a married man."

"I'm not taking a moral high ground," I murmured even though she was right. Pastor Brown down at the Sleepy Hollow Baptist Church would definitely not agree with Charlotte's behavior. "What did you do all those years in Sunday School and Sunday morning church, not to mention Wednesday night suppers?"

My mouth kept going like it had its own gears.

"I listened." Charlotte shrugged. "I guess now my legacy is going to be the cheating Raines."

"Maybe not. Maybe I should confess to me being a nun." I laughed. I looked in my rearview mirror when a motorcycle pulled up. The squirrely Dennis boy was on the back and he got off. The driver knocked the kickstand down and cut the engine. "Looks like we have company."

I sat for a moment calculating what my next move was. I watched the Dennis boy look in the back of the hearse; he obviously didn't know I was there. The driver got off the motorcycle and unsnapped the helmet, pulling it off, and the black frizzy hair sprung out like a spring. I knew I should be surprised that it was Princess Candy, but she was as manly as they came without being a man. She definitely wore the pants in the relationship.

"Who's in there, Dale?" Candy asked with a twang. "It ain't Mama, is it?"

"I don't see nothin'." His head jerked side to side like a chicken pecking for seeds.

"Well, shit." Candy put the helmet under her armpit and put the other hand on her hip. "You go right now and find out who is dead. You hear me?"

Dale Dennis hung his head. I opened the door and popped out, the file in my grip.

"Hi there." I smiled my sweetest southern smile, hoping Candy didn't recognize me. "I'm from Hardgrove's." I held the folder up. It made me feel a little less of a liar, as though I had proof. "I wanted to go over the wedding plans."

Candy rubbed her belly as she eyed me. Her jaw moved front to back, her lips side to side, before she opened her lips and used her tongue to make a suction noise against her teeth.

Dale Dennis stepped up. He pushed back his loose curly hair. "Umm, we didn't know anyone was comin'."

"Yeah, that's right." Candy stepped up next to her man, a foot taller than him. She planted her elbow on Dale's scrawny shoulder. "Me and Dale ain't got no business with the Hardgroves until they get things straight."

Candy glanced over my shoulder. She lifted her chin in the air.

"What's with the hearse?" She squinted. "It ain't like we got a dead body in there."

"It was the only company car left to take. You know I'm not using my own car for work." I knew I was going to have to get on their level. I opened the file. "I just wanted to come by and make sure that everything got squared away since I understand you had a little spat with your coordinator, Charlotte Raines."

Dale pulled out a cigarette from behind his ear. He took a lighter from his pocket and lit the smoke. Candy wacked him with the back side of her hand and nodded her head toward me.

"I don't recall a spat." He took a long draw off the cigarette. "The way we see it"—smoke came out with every word—"my Candy wants a wedding of a lifetime and I'm gonna give her what she wants. If she wants goats, she gets goats."

"Goats." Candy smiled. "Could you imagine us with fainting goats and little crowns of flowers around their cute itty-bitty heads?"

"That wouldn't work." I shook my head.

"I said"—Dale's voice escalated—"if my woman wants faintin' goats, she's gonna git faintin' goats."

"Why wouldn't it work?" She pushed herself and her protruding belly in front of Dale.

"The goats would eat all those fancy flowers you've ordered." I tapped the file.

"You are so good." Charlotte smiled. "Maybe you should add a wedding package at Eternal Slumber. You have a knack. Plus, you could use the inn as a reception hall."

"Oh," Candy snarled. She smacked poor old Dale on the arm again. "See, I told y'all there was a reason Charlotte had them stinkin' flowers there. But no, you had to get all . . ."

"What's goin' on out here?" The front door slammed shut and Melinda stood on the porch. She looked at the hearse and stepped off the four-by-four slab porch. "Is somethin' wrong with the baby?"

As she got closer, I saw she had something strapped around her waist. A fanny pack of sorts.

"Wait, find out what Candy was going to say to Dale." Charlotte stomped.

"What were you going to say about the stinkin' flowers?" I quickly asked, trying to beat the answer out of them before Melinda got there.

"Nothin'." Dale put his hand on Candy's belly. She smacked it away.

"I done warned you to stay away from me. You did this shit." Candy pointed to her stomach. "No nookie until after the baby."

"What about our wedding night?" he whined.

"You see this?" She swung her belly side to side. "Does it look like I want you to jump on this? No."

"When was the last time you talked to Charlotte?" I asked.

"Why you want to know? And who are you?" Melinda's brown eyes lowered. "What do you want?"

"Mama, go on inside. You don't feel good today. If you up and die, where am I and this rug rat going to go?" Candy stopped talking when Melinda twirled around and looked at her.

"You go on in the house and put them feet up. They are looking like sausages." Melinda pointed to the house. Her stern voice made me shimmy shake and be thankful she wasn't my mama. She moved her stare to Dale Dennis. "You too. Go on."

When Dale and Candy were safely in the house, Melinda turned to face me.

"Now, you and I both know that you are here for other reasons. I remember you from the wedding place. I already told them people you work for that I am not going to have my Candy's wedding at your facility and it stinkin' like the dead. So if you ain't here to give me my deposit back," Melinda snarled, "I suggest you get on out of here. You hear?" She bent over and held her stomach like she'd done at Hardgrove's that day.

"Can I ask what is wrong with you?" Curiosity

got to me. She clearly wasn't well and her face was grayer than I remembered.

"I got kidney failure and liver damage." Her head jerked side to side. "I wanted to do right by my baby and give her a wedding to be proud of, but it don't look like I'm gonna make it that long to see it. So I figured I'd just give her and that baby of hers the money to keep going without me."

"Gosh. I'm sorry to hear that." I shuffled my feet. I wasn't good with the living ill; I was good with the already dead ill. I never had the right words. "If you have any needs, I'd be glad to help."

"I've done had my gut full of you people. I done told you that I wasn't going to be needing your services. Not a wedding and certainly not my dead bed. Now get on out of here before I call the cops!" she yelled and pointed me out of the subdivision.

"You need somethin', mama?" Candy's protruding belly popped out of the screen door. Scrawny Dennis boy peeped over her shoulder.

"Call the poe-leece!" Melinda yelled over her shoulder. The screen door slammed shut. "You go on and git outta here."

That was all I needed to hear to jump back in the hearse. The last thing I wanted was Jack finding out that I had been arrested for bothering these people.

My phone rang and I pulled it out of my pocket. Mary Katherine Hardgrove was calling.

"Hello?" I quickly answered in case she decided to hang up on me before I could answer.

"You need to forget you talked to me." Her voice was deep and low. "I'll deny seeing you, and trust me when I say that your name will be erased from any file at Stevon's. I can make that happen and will," she threatened.

"Why the change of heart?" I asked.

"Let me tell you something." She was going to tell me whether I wanted to hear it or not. "My husband did not kill your sister. The cops have already let him go and I'm sticking by him. Your two-bit sister is the one who seduced my man and she got what was coming to her so you leave me and my family out of it."

"You wait one second, lady," I warned. "Sammy Hardgrove has been chasing my sister around like a sniffing dog for years. He might not have killed her but I won't stand by while you or any other Hardgrove try to drag her name through the mud because your husband couldn't keep his hands off her."

The phone clicked. I gripped the wheel wondering what had changed her mind. Who had changed her mind. Gina Marie Hardgrove.

Chapter 15

On my way back into Sleepy Hollow, I decided to stop by the Buy-N-Fly to get some cat food. I couldn't figure out what the cat wanted from me and it never wanted to stay around. It's not like I could talk to it like I could my other Betweener clients, so I couldn't help but think some sort of food might keep it around.

Everett Atwood jumped out of the metal chair when he saw me pull in. He grabbed the old oily rag off the back of the chair and stuffed it in the back of his pocket. He pointed me to the side of the gas pump where he could access the gas tank. I didn't need gas, but Everett took pride in his job of pumping gas, wiping the windows and making small talk.

"Mornin', Emma Lee." He opened the hearse door. He plucked the oily rag from his back pocket and snapped it. "Glad to see you didn't jump the curb today."

"You know that cat I saw?" I knew it was the ghost cat, but if I was buying cat food, he'd see it and this way I looked sane. He nodded and made circles with the cloth on my windshield. "I'm feeding it."

"You are?" Everett looked at me with narrowed eyes.

"Yes. And I'm going to run inside to get some cat food." I darted around the front of the hearse.

"You might want to get that salmon in gravy kind. Cats loves that stuff," Everett said and went on about his job.

Within minutes I had paid for my can of cat food, salmon in gravy, and gone back out to the car.

"This sure is a nice hearse." Everett wiped down the side. "You use it to carry people home?"

By home, I knew he meant to the cemetery.

"I do." The tone in his voice told me he had some questions. "Everett, do you need to ask me something?"

"Well," he tugged the ratty baseball hat off his head and tucked it up under his armpit. "I was wondering if I could talk to you about some funeral arrangements for me."

"You mean pre-need arrangements?" I asked.

"Something like that." He shuffled his feet around me and took the pump out of the gas tank and replaced it in the station.

"I thought you were a Burns man." I gripped the can of cat food and remembered all the rumors swirling around about the Ridley man's hat and Peggy's pearls.

A car zoomed in the gas station and the tires rolled over the water hose dingy bell.

"I'll have to talk to you later." Everett rushed over to the car and plucked the oily rag out of his back pocket to begin on the customer.

"Well, you are just racking up the dead." Charlotte was in the passenger side of the hearse. She was completely turned around in the seat looking back at Everett. "That was strange of him to ask all secret-like."

"I don't think so." I looked both ways before I pulled the hearse back out on the old country road. "He's very shy and if what you said about Burns getting all mixed up with clients and how you got Bea Allen's clients . . ." My mind took over and it automatically came out of my mouth, "Then Bea Allen is mad at you and she could've possibly killed you."

"Emma!" Charlotte squealed in delight, nearly causing me to hit a pedestrian that was crossing the sidewalk when I turned right, next to the town square.

My tires skidded to a stop. The person held his heart, and his eyes popped open.

Charlotte laughed and it was contagious. I started to laugh.

"I bet not many people have been almost hit by a hearse. I mean—" Charlotte stuttered through her giggles, as she pointed at the man. "People get hit by cars, but a hearse?"

When the man gave us the one finger salute, it made me laugh harder and my eyes teared from laughing. It took a minute for both of us to get our wits about us and for me to drive the few more feet to Eternal Slumber.

"This is so much fun." Charlotte straightened back up. She adjusted herself to where she was sitting slightly facing me. "I really do regret not taking time to really get to know you."

A lump formed in my throat. It was the opportunity I had been looking for. The perfect time to tell Charlotte exactly how I felt about how she'd treated me all my life. My heart pumped and the speech I had practiced so many times was on the tip of my tongue. I opened my mouth and it was just like something lifted off me. I closed my mouth and looked at her. The corners of her eyes dipped down, but her lips curled up.

"We have now." Words that I never practiced or ever intended to say to her spewed out of me. "Besides, you are my big sister. Who on earth wants to hang out with their little sister?"

"You really are a class act, Emma Lee." Charlotte ghosted out of the hearse and I got out.

Jack Henry was sitting in the family room of my apartment.

"Where have you been all day?" he asked while he tied up his tennis shoes. His baseball bag was sitting next to the couch. Whenever the Eternal Slumber softball team had practice and he had to work, he would put his bag in his cruiser and come to my house to change.

"Around." I shrugged and put the can of cat food on the coffee table. "Since you put the kibosh on me about Charlotte, I figured I'd spend a little time with the ghost cat and figure out what he needs."

"Did you ever think it just got hit by a car?" he asked.

"That's mean." My brows cocked. "And he seems to be looking for something or someone."

The images of Cat running around sniffing the shoes of the people in the town square made me think he was looking for that scent he remembered. If I could gain his trust, then maybe he'd lead me to where he'd come from. I'd heard so many stories about how animals get lost and find their way home years later. Why not ghost cats?

"And the can of cat food?" He stood up. He had on tight blue baseball pants. My heart went pitter-patter and my toes tingled. "Eyes up here, Emma."

I looked up and he was smiling.

"You are distracting." I curled up on my toes and kissed him. I made a little kissy path along his jaw and around to his ear. I whispered, "Are you sure you can't skip practice? Or be a few minutes late?"

An audible groan gurgled deep within him. I could tell he was thinking about it because of his pause.

"I think you need a nice rubdown so you will be ready for the game." I continued my little kissing path down and across his neck to the other ear. I took a little nibble on his lobe, knowing it would send him over the edge.

"You know I can't let the guys down," he whispered back and picked me up in his arms. I wrapped my arms around his neck and continued to snuggle while he carried me to the bedroom. Gently he laid me down and looked deep into my eyes.

The next few minutes was time well spent with Jack. It helped relieve some of the stress brought on by the past few days.

"You be a good girl until I get back." He pulled his shirt back over his head and stood up with an evil grin on his face.

"What?" I propped myself up on my elbows and watched him walk toward the door.

"Gotta go." He grabbed the baseball bag on the floor. "Don't forget our dinner date."

"I won't." I grabbed my pillow and threw it at him when he disappeared into the hall. I curled the other pillow in my arms and smiled. No matter how crazy my life was, and the pain I knew was coming my way with the realization that I'd not see or talk to Charlotte after she crossed over, I was blessed to have Jack in my life.

The soft sound of the cat paws pitter-pattered on the bedroom hardwood floors. The cat jumped up on the bed and looked at me.

"Here, kitty, kitty." I encouraged the cat to come closer. "I wish I knew your name."

The cat cautiously eased up next to me and kneaded the bed while a deep purr roared through its little body.

"You are my first animal. And I have a can of food for you." I sat up and called for the kitty. I was happy to see that it had followed me into the kitchen after I retrieved the can from the family room coffee table.

When I popped the can lid, the suction sound

sent the cat on its paws, dancing around, its tail dancing in the air.

"Oh, you like this food." I was happy that I had something to connect me with the ghost cat. "There is plenty more where this came from if you continue to stay around or lead me to places that will help me help you cross over."

I dumped the contents of the can on a paper plate and put it on the floor like it was going to eat it up. I was banking on the trust connection that might bring us together. Cats were a little skittish and the ghost cat was no different.

"What is that smell?" Mary Anna Hardy walked into the kitchen with her Marilyn Monroe coffee cup dangling from her finger. Her hair was short, curled and styled just like her favorite movie star icon. The black wrap dress was wrapped so tight around her, the girls bounced with each breath she took.

"It's cat food." I pointed to the plate. If I'd known someone was still here, I would've put the cat food in my apartment.

She pinched her nose with her fingers and waved her other hand in front of her to get the stink away. "Why?" Her voice nasal as she continued to plug her nose.

"I'm doing a sort of experiment," I lied. I was getting pretty good at covering up the Betweener gig. At first I admit I wasn't so good and was all willy-nilly when I spoke in public to my ghost clients and didn't realize how crazy I looked. "I have a client request to have cat food stuck in the casket along with ashes of a cat. It's a pre-need arrangement." My nose curled. The smell was awful.

"Who?" Mary Anna's excitement rushed up from the tips of her high heels and, like a wave, swooshed up her body and lit her face up. "I bet it's Dottie Kramer. She's got all them damn cats in that barn of hers. Is it?"

"I can't tell you." Happily the cat was still there. Normally, it would have darted off when Mary Anna walked in. I watched as the ghost cat danced and purred around the food. "But I'm not sure if I would agree to have the food at the funeral. Very foul." I waved my hand in front of my nose for more of an effect. "What are you doing here?"

"I left my good shears here from Sissy's funeral and I need to get them for work tomorrow. I also left my cup down there." She sighed. No matter how long I have lived, all my life, I still couldn't drink or eat anything down in the morgue. Not my Granny—she'd host a full buffet using her china down there if she could. "You want to go grab a beer at The Watering Hole?"

"No wonder you are all dolled up." I couldn't resist bringing attention to her outfit.

"I'm tired of being alone," she said. The sadness in her eyes spoke to me. "But you can't worry about that, honey."

I wasn't sure what to say. I'd never seen Mary Anna react this way to her single life. When I got my hair done, which was not on a regular basis, she always said how she was a strong woman, didn't need a man, wasn't looking for a man, just liked to love 'em and leave 'em.

"How are your mama and them?" she asked and stuck her cup on the counter.

"They don't know about Charlotte yet." I tried not to laugh as the cat rubbed his tail along Mary Anna's legs.

"What?" Her brows furrowed.

"They retired and lost their minds. They've been traveling the world and now they are in Africa on some safari where there is no human contact. They should be making a stop today at some internet café and the person who booked their tour said they would get the message to them." I wondered how Mom was going to react. When it did hit her, I was sure she'd act like one of them tigers she'd be seeing on her safari and claw her way to get home as fast as she could. "Then it will take her at least a couple of days to get to an airport and then God knows how long to get here."

"Is that why we haven't gotten started on her yet?" Mary Anna asked.

"No way in hell is she touching me." Charlotte appeared. "She puts on that music and shimmy shakes all over the place when she's doing a body. I just want minimal makeup and my hot-pink suit that's in my office at Hardgrove's."

"I'm sure we will get her soon." I forced a thin-lined grin on my face. I had meant to ask Jack to call since I'd been banned from Hardgrove's. Now that Charlotte's death was officially a homicide, then hopefully we could get her home soon.

Mary Anna's phone chirped and I gave Charlotte the big eyes to shut her up. It was hard to be present and listen to the living when the dead were always interrupting.

Charlotte bent down and picked up the cat.

"Oh, that's how you play this. I get no say in what I wear." She rubbed her hand down the cat. "Good, baby. We will find your mommy."

"Mommy?" I asked out loud and bit my lip when I realized I said it out loud.

Mary Anna hooked the bottom of her phone around her chin. "No, Bea Allen," she whispered.

"Bea Allen?" The cat leapt out of Charlotte's arms before she folded them in front of her. "That's weird. Why would Bea Allen be calling Mary Anna?" Her brows rose an inch.

I patiently waited until Mary Anna hung up.

"What was that about?" I asked.

"She's going to meet me at The Watering Hole." She avoided looking at me.

"Spill it," I spat. "I know better than that."

It wasn't that Mary Anna and Bea Allen were enemies, they weren't, but they definitely weren't friends. Mary Anna's mama, Leotta Hardy, and Bea were friends, which made this so much more interesting.

"Fine." Mary Anna stomped. "It's a favor for Mama. Bea Allen is having a hard time at Burns."

"Hard time?" I questioned.

"Oh, don't seem so smug." Mary Anna smiled. "Only if Charlotte was here to see this." She winked. I gulped. Charlotte about shit her pants.

"What?" Charlotte's mouth fell open. I wanted to take my finger and push it closed and tell her it wasn't polite to stand with your mouth open. Bad manners. "What does she mean?"

"I'm sure Charlotte is looking down on us." I looked up to the heavens and smiled.

"After how she treated you like a second-rate citizen in your own business, it has to feel good that your only competition in town has pretty much screwed up every single funeral she's done since O'Dell became mayor." Mary Anna shrugged.

"It was my understanding that most of those people went to Lexington to Hardgrove's." I told her what Charlotte told us not to say to anyone, but she was dead and it wasn't like her gossiping was going to overshadow the fact she was sleeping with a married man.

"Nothing against Charlotte, but I heard at the shop that Charlotte was just too expensive and she wasn't going to give a friend discount like y'all do around here. People appreciate that, Emma Lee." Mary always got the good gossip at her salon.

I swear, I think there was something hair stylists used to pump through their shops because as soon as your butt hit the plastic styling chairs, mouths flew open and puked out gossip whether it was true or not. Then it got twisted even more.

"It's a business." Charlotte threw her hands up in the air. "I'm not the owner there." Suddenly as if Charlotte's brain stopped, she looked at me, the skin between her eyes creased. She pointed at me. "Is that why we hardly made any money? Were you giving people discounts?"

I tucked my hand in the crook of Mary Anna's arm and started to walk her out of the kitchen and down the hall. It was time for her to leave because I had to talk to the cat while he was there, and Charlotte was getting madder.

"I had heard that Ridley had on Peggy Wayne's pearls and she had on his hat." I shook my head. "How do you mess that up?"

"You mean like the pin on Sissy?" Mary Anna threw it back in my face. She waved her hand in front of her as if she could just push her comment aside. "She said that she's ready for a drink because she's recovered a lot of the clients back and then some."

"Then some?" Charlotte questioned and eyed me suspiciously.

I opened the door. "Have fun."

"I will." She drummed her fingertips in the air behind her shoulder as she skipped down the front steps of the funeral home.

I turned around and Charlotte was sitting on top of the sideboard. She ran her hand across the top.

"I guess I won't get my hands on this." She lightly patted the top.

My phone chirped in my back pocket. I took it out. It was a text from Arley Burgin apologizing for texting me and that he'd gotten my number from John Howard. He wanted to know if I could make it out to the field to get their order that I had promised. I quickly texted back that I'd be out there before practice ended.

"Are you listening to me about this sideboard?"

Charlotte swung her legs back and forth. Her elbows were stiff, and her shoulders curled up to her ears from where she had her hands planted next to her.

"It doesn't matter now." I wasn't going to go there with her. "I wonder what Bea Allen meant when she told Mary Anna 'and then some'?"

How many new clients was she talking about?

There was something fishy and it wasn't just the smell of the can of cat food.

Chapter 16

The can of cat food didn't help me get any answers from the cat or clues to what it needed from me. The cat did stay around a little bit longer and allowed me to pet him a couple of times but not as long as he let Charlotte. I guess that was the beginning of trust.

"What do you think Bea Allen did to get new clients?" I asked Charlotte when we went back to my apartment.

She sat down on the couch next to me and the cat sat in her lap.

"I don't know." She sighed and picked at the cat's loose fur. "I guess you could go look at her files or something since she is going to The Watering Hole."

I turned my head toward her and a smile eased upon my lips.

"I could just make a pit stop since I do need to go by Softball Junction like I promised Arley." The plan could work. Burns Funeral wasn't in the town square; it was clear on the other side of town and if Bea Allen wasn't there, that meant it was empty, unless there were a dead body or two.

I glanced up at the clock. I had plenty of time to snoop around and see what I could find out.

"Let's go." I jumped up and grabbed the keys of the hearse.

Within a couple of minutes, Charlotte and I were walking down the sidewalk near Burns Funeral. I didn't park directly in front or in the driveway in case someone noticed. If someone saw the hearse parked in front of a house, they would think I was there to collect someone or just visiting for arrangements. I walked around the funeral home to see if I saw any motion or lights inside and walked to the service entrance on the side when I felt like the coast was clear.

Burns Funeral Home building was really no different than Eternal Slumber. Both were very old Victorian homes turned into funeral homes. The stately brick houses had wonderfully large rooms with big windows, perfect for layouts. The crown molding was something new buildings didn't have; they could try to duplicate but it didn't add the same character. The character added to the feel of the importance of a nice send-off. Just like Eternal Slumber, there was a large front porch with a fence. Burns had yellow brick and white trim; Eternal Slumber had red brick with white trim. Both were beautiful, but the employees and owners were quite different.

"Why are you going in this way?" Charlotte asked.

"When Mamie and I had to get her teeth, she told me to go in this side because it's always left open." I recalled Mamie Sue Preston, one of my Betweener clients who had been killed over money. Mamie's false teeth were supposed to go with her in her casket, but the Burns people had left them in her file. She was insistent that I get her teeth and stick them in her casket. Her buried casket.

Lucky for me, Mamie had one of those old-time bells on top of her tombstone that had a string going down into the earth and into a tiny hole in her casket. She was a hypochondriac and said she wanted the string in case she was buried alive and could pull the string to ding the bell to alert the living that she'd been buried alive. I was able to slip the dental plate into the ground through the hole the string was hanging through, making Mamie a happy Betweener customer.

"Now what?" Charlotte bounced on her toes. There was excitement in her eyes.

"Calm down." I laughed. I couldn't help but wonder if this Charlotte was somewhere buried under the Charlotte she put on display for the world to see.

"Emma Lee Raines, you are getting sneakier than Granny." Charlotte smiled. "She used to drag me around and sneak in here when I was a kid."

"She did?" Charlotte could've knocked me over with a feather. She nodded her head. "You never told me that."

"There are a lot of things I didn't tell you about me and Granny." She turned her fingers in front of her mouth like she was locking it. "Tick-a-lock."

We both laughed at one of Granny's old sayings when Granny couldn't keep a secret for the life of her.

The sunlight was fading fast. I still had to get to the softball field. I took my phone out of my back pocket and used the flashlight instead of turning on the lights once I got into Bea's office. I didn't want to bring any attention to me.

There was a bag from the same undertaker convention in Des Moines that Sammy Hardgrove

was going to use as a cover-up for his rendez-
vous with Charlotte. I picked up the photo booth
photo Bea Allen had taken with a group of other
conference goers with the date and time stamp of
around the time Charlotte was killed.

"Look." I held the photo up. "Bea was at the
convention."

"Good for her," Charlotte snarked.

"It means she didn't kill you even though she
said she'd get you back for taking her clients." I
took a deep breath. Not that I was unhappy Bea
Allen Burns hadn't killed Charlotte, but the two
main suspects I had had true alibis. "It looks like
we are starting from ground zero."

"Aren't you still going to look around?" Charlotte asked.

"Maybe just to be nosy and see who 'and then
some' are." The curiosity was getting to me while
I was in here so I might as well do a little snooping. Besides, it was good gossip for Granny when
she felt better.

The files were still in the metal cabinet like
they'd been the last time I had broken in. There
was a new box of yellow files on her desk and
a hole punch as if she were working on files. I
waved the flashlight over the paperwork and immediately noticed Cheryl Lynne Doyle's name.

"No." I grabbed the paper and took a closer look. "No way."

The thought that Cheryl Lynne would switch funeral homes, not that she was already with me at Eternal Slumber, but we were friends. Good friends. The Doyles were Eternal Slumber people, not Burns.

"Well, well, well." Charlotte stood behind me. "I thought Granny said you were five bodies deep."

"I am busy." I put Charlotte aside and tried to wrap my brain around why Cheryl Lynne would not only make pre-need arrangements at Burns, but at her age.

She and I were just a couple years apart and she was younger than me. She was in her mid-twenties. Were her parents' pre-needs here?

I scurried over to the filing cabinet and dragged my finger down the front until I reached the D drawer for Doyle. The metal wheels screeched when I pulled the drawer to full extension. My fingers danced along the top tabs of the files.

"D-O," I repeated until I got to the D-O's. "D-O-Y-L-E." There weren't that many people in Sleepy Hollow with the last name of Doyle and not in the filing system either.

"Emma," Charlotte called. She was still standing over the desk looking down at the files. "I think you want to look at this."

Satisfied there were no Doyles in the filing cabinet, I walked back over and looked at what Charlotte was pointing to. It was a copy of Cheryl's driver's license.

"It's her license," I said in a no-big-deal way. "You know that every funeral home requires different forms of ID." I winked and joked, "In Hardgrove's case it just so happens that you have to sacrifice your next of kin."

"Not next of kin. Try next kidney." Charlotte bit the side of her lip. "I think I know what's going on."

"Huh?" I looked back down at Cheryl's driver's license where Charlotte was tapping her finger.

"The little round black circle is really the orange organ donation sticker they give you at the DMV when you sign up for organ donation." She slid her eyes up to mine and her stare sent a chill down my spine. "It shows up black when you photocopy the license.

"I'm an organ donor." I wasn't following what Charlotte was saying.

"Emma." Slowly, Charlotte's chin lifted. Her mouth dropped open, and she had tears on the rims of her eyelids. She gulped. "I think I know who killed me and why."

"Tell me." I begged her before she ghosted away. "Charlotte, get back here," I demanded and jerked around the room.

I called for her a few times on the way out of the funeral home and grumbled down the sidewalk when I realized she wasn't around.

The entire ride over to the softball field I thought about what had just transpired. First off, Cheryl Lynne was going to donate organs. That wasn't a big deal, but something about seeing those files triggered something in Charlotte that made her believe she knew what was going on. Sammy was off the hook and Bea Allen was no longer a suspect, so who and why? Nothing was coming to me.

Charlotte Rae was going to have to show up and tell me what she was thinking. I had no other leads.

The lights around the field were on and Jack Henry loved that. He said that there was nothing better than playing under softball lights. The team had on their old uniforms from last year, but they still looked good.

Jack jogged over when he saw me standing at the fence. My heart jumped seeing him coming toward me, propelling me back into high school. He would jog over to the fence and talk to Jade Lee Peel, his high school girlfriend and my last Betweener client, say a few words to her and jog away. There were so many times I had pretended to be her; not so much now since she's six feet under and I was standing there.

"Hey." He curled his fingers around my fingers as they stuck through the fence. "How's it going?"

Without saying it, I knew he meant Charlotte.

"I don't know." I shook my head and saw Arley walking over. "She said something about knowing who killed her and why. Then poof." I puffed my fingers out like fireworks, acting like Charlotte disappeared into thin air.

"Ms. Raines." Arley took his hat off. "You here to make good on your promise?"

"I sure am." I smiled. "And to talk to you about making an appointment for some information."

"Yeah." He looked down and used the toe of his cleat to move dirt around.

"I'll see you for dinner?" Jack asked and squeezed my fingers. It hurt a little bit, but I didn't care.

"Sounds good," I said and turned my attention to Arley. "Can you get the sizes of the guys and some equipment you might need and I'll get it ordered?"

"Sure. Doc gave me some bad news about my dad and I want to make sure I get things all cleared up." He looked up. His eyes were sad.

"You don't want to use Hardgrove's?" The question was reasonable.

"I . . . um . . ." His hesitation only made me more curious.

"You what?" I asked. "Do you know something about Charlotte's death?"

"No!" He was quick and loud. "I mean, no. I just don't know what kind of mood they are in since her death. I mean, it's like business as usual. Even Mrs. Hardgrove is in there."

"Mrs.? As in the mom?" It had been years since I'd seen her.

"Mrs. Mary Katherine Hardgrove." Hearing her name sent a jolt to my gut. Mary Katherine was not an undertaker. "She's like living there. Going through everything as if she owns the place."

The softball field spun around me. The lights were like a spotlight on Arley and me. "Mary Katherine? As in Sammy's wife?" Suddenly all the air left my body and I started to gasp.

"Are you okay, Ms. Raines?" Arley asked.

"Yeah, yeah." I waved my hand in front of me. I couldn't help but wonder what deal Gina Marie had given Mary Katherine. If Mary Katherine had taken over Charlotte's job already, she had something to blackmail Gina Marie and vice versa.

"When I hired you, I told him to stay far away from this location. And now he tells me he is leaving his wife, which will put a piece of Hardgrove's hard-earned dollars in her hands. Something I cannot let happen. Does this have anything to do with you? Because I swear if it does, you'll regret it! Plus, you need to sign off on those

papers your crazy sister was flapping her lips about because you are in breach of contract."

I gulped. Had Charlotte remembered something about Gina Marie and her job when we were at Burns? It only made sense.

"Anyways, if my dad doesn't get a lung soon, then he is going to die." Arley's lips turned down.

"Oh. He's on the donor list?" Donor list? When we saw the donor sticker at Burns Funeral Home, Charlotte went blank and that was when she disappeared. "I'm sorry, Arley, but I've got to get going." I walked backward toward the hearse. "Let me know what I can do for you!" I called out.

Charlotte was at Hardgrove's Legacy Center. I could feel it . . . in my organs.

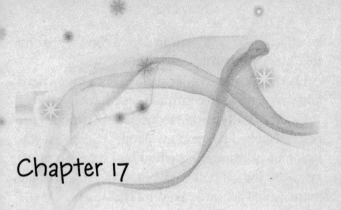

Chapter 17

My phone chirped in a text while I was zip-
ping out of Sleepy Hollow and heading back
to Lexington. Specifically, Hardgrove's Legacy
Center. If my hunches were right, then I knew exactly why Charlotte Rae was killed, but not sure by
who. The only person who truly wasn't accounted
for on the morning of Charlotte's death was Gina
Marie. She loved her family. She loved her family
business. And she loved the life she lived. It only
seemed right to get rid of someone who was going
to change that for you. In Gina Marie's case it was
Charlotte because Charlotte held the key to Sammy's divorce, and no one had anything to gain
from a divorce but Mary Katherine Hardgrove. By
eliminating Charlotte, Gina Marie's life would not

be affected . . . until Sammy got a conscience and told Mary Katherine everything.

I had the entire scenario played out in my head and I was going to confront Gina Marie.

I waited until I made it to the gates of Hardgrove's before I looked down at my phone. I figured it was Jack Henry wondering why I had scurried off so fast from the softball field, but it wasn't. It was my mom. My heart sank. Before I had read her text, I knew she knew about Charlotte.

She said that they didn't have calling service and she'd had to be seen by a doctor when she got news about Charlotte. She and Daddy were on an elephant's back and trying to get to civilization as quick as the damn lump could get them there—her words not mine. Her travel agent had booked them on the red-eye back to the United States and they would be here as soon as they could, which was probably going to be another thirty-six hours. She asked to keep Charlotte and the funeral arrangements open until she and Daddy got back.

I simply texted back that I loved them and to be safe. I was taking care of everything and I'd be sure to keep Charlotte above ground until they got home. Little did they know, I couldn't even get Charlotte, but I was determined to have this wrapped up before Momma and Daddy got home.

The parking lot was empty except for the security guy's car, so I parked around back next to the Dumpster. Somehow I had to get in Hardgrove's to take a look at Charlotte's body, get the papers she had for me in the top drawer and grab her outfit from her closet.

There was a lot of work to do in very little time and, without her help, it was going to prove difficult.

There were several service doors around the back of Hardgrove's. Most of them were probably emergency exits from the banquet rooms and other behind-the-scenes rooms like the kitchen.

Headlights darted down the side of the building and I took cover behind a Dumpster. The lights turned the corner and a white van barreled down, passing me and stopping a couple doors down. The man got out of the van and walked up to the door, giving it a good hard knock.

The security guard stepped out and said a few things before he gave the man the go-ahead and propped the door open. The van driver walked to the back of the van and opened both doors. He let down a little ramp and rolled out one of those industrial linen baskets on wheels. When both men were inside, I tiptoed at a fast pace, hoping to get inside. The van had a dry cleaning logo on it. It wasn't unusual for these bigger companies to come after hours to get the linens like the slipcovers, casket covers, table covers, along with all the other linens they used from all the other parties they hosted here.

Before I could make it to the door, I heard them talking and getting closer. I ran to the back of the van and climbed in. There were several other baskets with fresh linens and some plastic bags with the hazardous symbol on them that we used during embalming. I jumped in one and shimmied my way to the bottom, moving around the plastic bags and covering my head with the clean linens.

"This is a heavy one." The van driver laughed. "Must be full of organs."

"Good." The security guard's shadow darted down into basket. "Get them out of here."

My body shifted to the side when the cart began to move. I tried to wedge myself with my feet and hands in a flat tent position. Thank God I was small.

Full of organs? Huh? Shouldn't it be full of clean linens and the hazardous bags we used for the organs to go out, not in?

The sound of the beeping elevator let me know we were getting on and going down to the morgue, which was exactly where I wanted to go and see Charlotte's body. It was one thing for the police not to release the body to the family because of the murder investigation, but another not to let us see her.

The bumpy ride ended about five minutes later and when the sound of footsteps was followed up by the clicking of the door, I knew the coast was clear. Before I even emerged from the basket, I could feel the cold temperature of the morgue.

I pushed myself up to get out of the basket and my hand landed on one of the plastic bags and something squishy. The ick factor made me move quicker and the shudder inside of me alerted me that something was very wrong with the linens.

I took my phone out of my pocket and turned on the flashlight, hovering it over and in the basket. With the light shining down, I moved a couple of the fresh linens and stared at the clear bags filled with some sort of blood. I bent down and picked up the bag and held it up in the air before I realized what it was.

"Oh my God." Heavy and deep sighs escaped my body when I realized what was going on at Hardgrove's.

"What's going on here?" The security guard had flipped on the light and found me standing there holding the fresh organ. Behind him was the dry cleaning guy with bags of ice propped up on his shoulder.

"I'm here to get my sister." My head turned

toward Charlotte's ghost, who was standing over her own body that was cut in a Y-formation with her blood circulating through a pump. My stomach curled. I felt dizzy and faint as I watched her body being kept warm for the organ extraction they were set to do to steal her organs.

"I remember." Charlotte's voice was low and sad.

"Now you remember," I said in a sarcastic tone and threw my hands in the air.

The men looked between each other.

"Who are you talking to?" the guard asked with a curious look in his eye.

"Her." I pointed to Charlotte. "Her ghost."

"You're nuts," the dry cleaning man scoffed. "She's nuts." He turned to the guard.

The guard kept his hand next to his hip.

Charlotte said, "I had a family that swore their sister was an organ donor and it was on our paperwork. When I went to get the paperwork, it was not on there. The security guard is the only person here at night and able to get into my office with his key. I was putting two and two together that he was going in and changing the organ donors to non-organ donors. He was stealing their organs and selling to the black market."

"I've seen her, so I'll be going." I smiled and hoped they were just going to let me go. I was wrong.

The security guard pulled his gun from under his shirt and pointed it at me. "I can't let you do that."

"Boss, she's going to rat us out." The other guy was a bit jumpy.

"Nah, she's trespassing. The Hardgroves don't want her on the property and it was filed with the police, so technically I could just shoot her saying she trespassed." He had a point. "Then we can put her body upstairs, clean up this mess and get on with our business."

"You honestly think that you are going to get away with harvesting people's organs and selling them?" The thought of them doing this made me sick.

"The liver you just had in your hands is going to a good woman. I'm saving lives." He smiled.

"You are stealing. How does Gina Marie not know this?" I questioned. "Or does she?"

"I walked in on him and Arley stealing the organs from the deceased even if they weren't organ donors and selling them to the black market." Charlotte was still standing over her body. "The other guy is Hardgrove's cleaning driver. The Hardgroves have him come at night and pick up the laundry. It makes it easy for him to transport the ice in, extract the organs, put them on ice and get them out without anyone noticing."

"That is what Gina Marie meant when she said that you needed to double-check the donation card when I thought she meant clothes, etc." It was all coming to me. Granted, it was coming to me at the absolute wrong time, but at least I was going to cross over with Charlotte knowing what exactly happened to her.

"And Arley Burgin?" I asked, shocked.

"What?" The security guard took a step forward. "Did Arley tell you about this?" He spat. "I told him to keep his big mouth shut."

"Why did you involve Arley?" I asked, dumbfounded that Arley would do such a thing.

"I needed eyes on the inside and his daddy needs a lung. When you're dying, you do desperate things to stay alive or keep the ones you love alive." He stepped closer, the gun still pointing at me. "Like right now, I bet you'd just about do anything to keep me from putting a piece of lead in you right now."

"You never said anything about us killing people." The van driver's face flushed pale. "You only said already dead people."

"Shut up, Jenkins!" the security guard screamed over his shoulder. "Shit happens. Things come up and plans change. Do you want to go to jail for the rest of your life or do you want her to go away as if this never happened?"

The van driver didn't say anything. The silence was deafening.

"Now." The security guard's voice had considerably calmed down and was steady. "I've got to decide what to do with you."

He took a walk around me and gave me a good once-over.

"You just might be the lung Arley's daddy needs." A slow, calculated smile curved on his lips. "See, it's not a bad thing that you will be joining your sister. She has a beautiful kidney that's going to get me thousands of dollars." He winked and shoved the gun in my side.

I winced from the pain of the barrel hitting my lower rib. I gulped. I'd done gotten myself into one hell of a situation.

"I don't think anyone is going to do anything anymore." Arley Burgin stood at the door like a knight in shining armor. "Pete, this is over. I can't let you do this to anyone else, even if my daddy don't get a lung."

"Shut the hell up, Arley, and get over here and tie her up with some of that rope over there before I gut you and give your daddy your own lung." Pete waved the gun. "Hurry up before anyone else shows up."

"I'm not going to do this." Arley held his ground.

"Fine. Your choice. Dan, do your job," Pete instructed Dan.

Dan hesitated and looked at Arley. Arley's chest puffed out like a puffer fish and he stood ramrod straight, preparing for Dan to hit him.

Suddenly a can was thrown into the room spewing all sorts of smoke.

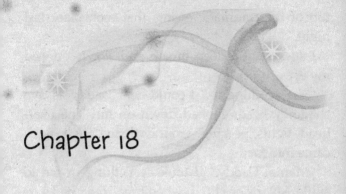

Chapter 18

That's her," I heard Charlotte say. "When she wakes up, she will see you and help you."

"Are you sure?" the small voice asked. "I've been waiting a very long time."

"I'm sure," Charlotte confirmed. "She's my sister. She's got a special gift. She can see us and help us go to the other side. I only wish I had known it while I was living."

The sound of footsteps came from the left and Charlotte stopped talking.

"Are you sure she's going to be okay?" The comforting and sweet voice of my mama asked.

"She will." Doc Clyde was standing next to me. "She's just got a case of the 'Funeral Trauma' on top of the traumatic events that took place last night."

I sucked in a deep breath and slowly opened my eyes.

"She's coming to." I could hear Daddy as two shadowy heads looked down on me. The overhead lights peering around them. Their faces came into focus.

"Mama, Daddy." It took everything in me to smile. My insides lit up when I realized I had survived Pete's gun. "Was I shot?"

"No, honey. Thank God," Mama cried and patted my hand. "I don't know what I'd have done if both my girls were gone."

"Move it." Granny shoved Mama to the side and looked at me. "You did it."

"I did what?" I asked confused.

"You saved Charlotte and a whole lot of other victims from the big organ scam." Granny scooched down a little to let Jack Henry in view.

A blanket of relief came over me when I saw him. Every single person I loved was standing in the room. Even Charlotte.

"I love you, Emma Lee." Jack bent down and kissed my lips. "You scared me to death, though." He put his hand on my forehead and ran it across the top of my head.

"Give the lovebirds some room." Granny shooed everyone out, including Doc.

"You're not mad?" I asked.

"I would be if you'd been seriously hurt." The chair legs screeched across the hospital tile floor as he dragged a chair next to me. "But you did a good thing."

"How did I get here?" I asked. The last thing I remembered was Pete's gun sticking in my side.

"It was Arley. After you left the softball field so abruptly, I got a little nervous. Arley asked me what was wrong and I just said that you were on edge because Hardgrove didn't let you see Charlotte yet." Jack shook his head. "He mumbled something about you being a good person and he couldn't do it to you. Then spilled his guts."

I started to remember everything with Pete and Dan while they had me at gunpoint.

"He said that he had told the security guard his daddy was going to need a lung transplant and that's how the plan was hatched. Arley was the inside eyes and he told the security guard everything about everyone's files. Arley would only give out information from the inside and the security guard would go in and change the files at night when no one was around. The laundry service driver even got involved by transporting

the organs where they needed to go. Since everything was done at night, he never got caught." Jack
rubbed his fingers against his thumb. "They were
getting upward of ten thousand dollars an organ."

"The price people pay." I couldn't believe it.

"Arley said that Charlotte had come in unex-
pectedly that night when Pete was harvesting and
she caught him with an organ. He strangled her
with some rope and dragged her outside behind
the bushes. That's why she's got dirt on her outfit.
Sammy Hardgrove had Arley go to his apartment
to fix a few things and that's how Arley knew
about the apartment. Pete had Arley convinced
the police would see Arley as the mastermind
since he was always in the building, so he used
that to manipulate Arley into doing whatever he
needed." Jack rubbed his hand up and down my
arm. "Arley was stuck in between a rock and hard
place because he really liked you and he wants his
dad to live. So he took the body and left her in the
apartment."

"Hard place?" I questioned. "He was doing il-
legal things."

"I know that and you know that, but in Arley's
world, he had to justify his actions somehow, so
when I said something at the softball field about
you not taking Charlotte's murder so good, he
came clean."

"I really thought Gina had done it." I bit my bottom lip wondering how wrong I was.

"She didn't. Nothing to do with it," Jack confirmed. "I think she's more shocked than any of us."

"How did you know I was there?" I asked.

"I jumped online and pinged your phone. I didn't want to call you and let your phone ring because I figured you'd gone and gotten yourself into a pickle." He smiled. "I called Lexington police and told them what was going on. They sent over the SWAT team and saw that linen van there, which Arley identified as the guy that actually did all the organ extraction, not only for Pete but also for another funeral home in Lexington. He was going to take out Charlotte's kidney but you ruined that."

"Thank goodness." I sat up in the hospital bed.

"Thank goodness he came clean and the SWAT threw in the can of tear gas."

"I remember now." I recalled the smoke. I shivered, thinking about how close I had come to becoming a Betweener client of my own. Jack took off his jacket and draped it over my shoulders. My heart warmed with his kind gesture. I was one lucky girl.

"The tear gas instantly knocked everyone out." He patted my leg.

"What about Arley?" I knew he was wrong and

what they had done was wrong, but he did save my life and Charlotte's organs.

"He will spend some time in jail and Pete was arrested on first degree murder charges along with gross misdemeanor of a corpse. Several corpses."

"It's time." Charlotte caught my attention and looked off into the distance.

"No, wait." I turned my attention to Charlotte. "No," I begged. A lump formed in my throat. A burning sensation collected on my eyelids and inside my mouth where my nose met my throat. "Please, don't go."

"Charlotte?" Jack asked. I nodded. "She's crossing over?"

I nodded again, barely seeing him through the puddle of tears in my eyes.

"I'll leave you alone for a minute." Jack quietly slipped out of the room and shut the door behind him. I knew he was going to not let anyone in and give me a minute with my sister.

"Please, no." I reached out and Jack's coat fell to the floor.

"Emma," Charlotte gasped and pointed to the coat.

There was a small velvet ring box that had fallen out of the pocket.

"It's a ring." Charlotte's eyes danced with delight. "You are going to get married."

"No." I gulped back the bittersweet moment. "Not without you by my side."

"I have to." Charlotte ghosted herself next to my bed. "I'm sorry for not being the big sister you wanted me to be. You are going to be a beautiful bride."

She pointed to the coat.

"Now pick it up and act like you don't know anything about it." She looked so angelic with the brightest smile across her face. Her eyes lit up like stars. "Let him wow you with how much he loves you and adores you."

I did what she asked me to do and put the coat on the edge of the bed.

"You are a great big sister." The tears flowed down my face. I extended my arm and held my fingers out to touch her. "Please, don't go. Please."

"It's a shame, you know. I helped families get their loved ones in the ground while you helped their loved ones cross over. We would've made a heck of a team. Now it's my turn." Charlotte took a step backward and looked over her shoulder. "I love you, Emma Lee. You remember that and take care of Granny."

"Wait," I sobbed as Charlotte faded away.

The pain struck deep in my heart and I fell back on the bed.

Jack Henry walked back in and crawled in the bed with me and held me tight, rocking me back and forth, comforting me as I mourned the loss of my sister.

A couple of hours later, Doc Clyde gave me my discharge papers because nothing was hurting but my heart. I was on the other side of the funeral business today. I was able to feel the pain my clients' families had as they would sit in front of me making the arrangements for their loved ones. In some sick way, this was probably going to make me a better undertaker. Be more sympathetic, in a way.

"This is the first time I've seen her grieve," Granny said in a hushed whisper as they rolled me down the hospital hall in the wheelchair Doc Clyde insisted I use to get to the car.

"We are here to help," Mama assured her.

As we passed the waiting room next to the nurses' station, I saw Princess Candy and the Dennis boy sitting in some chairs.

"Wait!" I put my foot down to stop the wheelchair. Slowly I got up so I wouldn't pass out and I walked over to them. "Is the baby okay?"

"The baby is fine." Candy rubbed her belly. "It's my mama. She got her kidney transplant today."

"Wonderful news." I clapped my hands together. "I'm so glad you didn't have that big wedding because now you can have your mama and your baby there."

"We can never thank you enough." The Dennis boy stood up and hugged me.

Like a breeze, Charlotte whispered into my ear, "I told you it was my turn to give back."

"Charlotte?" I questioned and put my hand up to my lips.

"Yes," Candy teared. "Your mama and daddy found those papers Charlotte had left for you. Somehow she knew her kidneys were supposed to go to my mama."

"Her lungs went to Arley's daddy." Jack patted my shoulders and had me sit back down in the wheelchair.

I had completely forgotten about the papers Charlotte had left. She must've known something fishy was going on in her morgue and written up her last will and testament before she'd gone down and seen the guard harvesting all the organs. But it all made sense now. As much as I wanted to mourn my sister's death, I knew that she had done a very good thing in the end that made up for all the bad things she'd done while living.

Even her funeral and repass was a celebration. The entire town square was filled with mourners coming to say their goodbyes. Charlotte Rae would've loved all the attention she was bringing to Eternal Slumber. When I was questioned about her epitaph choice of words *It's My Turn*, I knew the real meaning behind it. Charlotte knew it was her turn to give back unselfishly, but the townsfolk thought it meant that Charlotte had put so many others in the ground that it was her turn to go into the ground.

I sat under the gazebo with the ghost cat next to me and watched the line of Sleepy Hollow citizens curl down the sidewalk and up the steps of the funeral home waiting their turn to get inside to pay their respects to Mama, Daddy and Granny.

"Here kitty, kitty." A familiar voice called and l looked up.

There was a young girl and a much older woman running after her.

The ghost cat jumped to its feet and stared at the young girl coming toward us.

"Kitty!" The girl outstretched her arms and ran as fast as she could. The cat darted off in her direction until it reached her. The young girl picked up the cat and hugged it tight.

"Put it down," the woman instructed the girl and looked up at me. "Lovely day, isn't it?" The woman adjusted the hem of her shirt.

"Not really." I pointed to the funeral home. "My sister's funeral."

"Oh, I'm so sorry to hear that." The woman was doing some very familiar hand gestures toward the girl and cat.

"He does love to aggravate you." The young girl laughed when she put the cat down and it tried to rub up on her leg.

I laughed.

"You." The young girl looked up at me. "You can help me."

"What?" the woman spat and looked up at me.

"She can see me. The ghost at the hospital told me." Then her voice hit me like a ton of bricks. When I was in the hospital, I vaguely remember Charlotte telling someone that I could help them cross over.

"No." The woman jerked. "She cannot help you."

"Yes, I can," I said to the woman. The cat ran over to me and sat down on the step. "Are you a Betweener?" I asked the woman. I'd never met someone with the same gift as me.

"She is, but she won't help me cross over. We are twins and I was murdered years ago. She says if she helps me, then she'll never see me again." The young girl begged, "Please, help me and Mr. Whiskers."

"So, you are Mr. Whiskers?" I ran my hand down Mr. Whiskers's fur before I glanced up at the little girl and her grown twin sister staring back at me.

"Well?" The little girl twirled her pigtail around her finger and dug the toe of her sandal in the dirt patch on the ground. "Are you going to help me or not?"

A GHOSTLY UNDERTAKING

A funeral, a ghost, a murder . . . It's all in a day's work for Emma Lee Raines. . . .

Bopped on the head from a falling plastic Santa, local undertaker Emma Lee Raines is told she's suffering from "Funeral Trauma." It's trauma all right, because the not-so-dearly departed keep talking to her. Take Ruthie Sue Payne—innkeeper, gossip queen, and arch-nemesis of Emma Lee's granny—she's adamant that she didn't just fall down those stairs. She was pushed.

Ruthie has no idea who wanted her pushing up daisies. All she knows is that she can't cross over until the matter is laid to eternal rest. In the land of the living, Emma Lee's high-school crush, Sheriff Jack Henry Ross, isn't ready to rule out foul play. Granny Raines, the widow of Ruthie's ex-husband and co-owner of the Sleepy Hollow Inn, is the prime suspect. Now Emma Lee is stuck playing detective or risk being haunted forever.

Another day. Another funeral. Another ghost.
Great. As if people didn't think I was freaky enough. But, truthfully, this was becoming a common occurrence for me as the director of Eternal Slumber Funeral Home.

Well, the funeral thing was common.

The ghost thing . . . that was new, making Sleepy Hollow anything *but* sleepy.

"What is *she* doing here?" A ghostly Ruthie Sue Payne stood next to me in the back of her own funeral, looking at the long line of Sleepy Hollow's residents that had come to pay tribute to her life. "I couldn't stand her while I was living, much less dead."

Ruthie, the local innkeeper, busybody and my

granny's arch-nemesis, had died two days ago after a fall down the stairs of her inn.

I hummed along to the tune of "Blessed Assurance," which was piping through the sound system, to try and drown out Ruthie's voice as I picked at baby's breath in the pure white blossom funeral spray sitting on the marble-top pedestal table next to the casket. The more she talked, the louder I hummed and rearranged the flowers, gaining stares and whispers of the mourners in the viewing room.

I was getting used to those stares.

"No matter how much you ignore me, I know you can hear and see me." Ruthie rested her head on my shoulder, causing me to nearly jump out of my skin. "If I'd known you were a light seeker, I probably would've been a little nicer to you while I was living."

I doubted that. Ruthie Sue Payne hadn't been the nicest lady in Sleepy Hollow, Kentucky. True to her name, she was a pain. Ruthie had been the president and CEO of the gossip mill. It didn't matter if the gossip was true or not, she told it.

Plus, she didn't care much for my family. Especially not after my granny married Ruthie's ex-husband, Earl. And *especially* not after Earl died and left Granny his half of the inn he and Ruthie had owned together . . . the inn where Granny and Ruthie both lived. The inn where Ruthie had died.

I glared at her. Well, technically I glared at Pastor Brown, because he was standing next to me and he obviously couldn't see Ruthie standing between us. Honestly, I wasn't sure there was a ghost between us, either. It had been suggested that the visions I had of dead people were hallucinations . . .

I kept telling myself that I was hallucinating, because it seemed a lot better than the alternative—I could see ghosts, talk to ghosts, be touched by ghosts.

"Are you okay, Emma Lee?" Pastor Brown laid a hand on my forearm. The sleeve on his brown pin-striped suit coat was a little too small, hitting above his wrist bone, exposing a tarnished metal watch. His razor-sharp blue eyes made his coal-black greasy comb-over stand out.

"Yes." I lied. "I'm fine." Fine as a girl who was having a ghostly hallucination could be.

"Are you sure?" Pastor Brown wasn't the only one concerned. The entire town of Sleepy Hollow had been worried about my well-being since my run-in with Santa Claus.

No, the spirit of Santa Claus hadn't visited me. *Yet.* Three months ago, a plastic Santa had done me in.

It was the darndest thing, a silly accident.

I abandoned the flower arrangement and smoothed a wrinkle in the thick velvet drapes, remembering that fateful day. The sun had been out, melting away the last of the Christmas snow. I'd decided to walk over to Artie's Meat and Deli, over on Main Street, a block away from the funeral home, to grab a bite for lunch since they had the best homemade chili this side of the Mississippi. I'd just opened the door when the snow and ice around the plastic Santa Claus Artie had put on the roof of the deli gave way, sending the five-foot jolly man crashing down on my head, knocking me out.

Flat out.

I knew I was on my way to meet my maker when Chicken Teater showed up at my hospital bedside. I had put Chicken Teater in the ground two years ago. But there he was, telling me all sorts of crazy things that I didn't understand. He blabbed on and on about guns, murders and all sorts of dealings I wanted to know nothing about.

It wasn't until my older sister and business partner, Charlotte Rae Raines, walked right through Chicken Teater's body, demanding that the doctor do something for my hallucinations, that I realized I wasn't dead after all.

I had been *hallucinating*. That's all. Hallucinating.

Doc Clyde said I had a case of the "Funeral Trauma" from working with the dead too long.

Too long? At twenty-eight, I had been an undertaker for only three years. I had been around the funeral home my whole life. It was the family business, currently owned by my granny, but run by my sister and me.

Some family business.

Ruthie tugged my sleeve, bringing me out of my memories. "And her!" she said, pointing across the room. Every single one of Ruthie's fingers was filled up to its knuckles with rings. She had been very specific in her funeral "pre-need" arrangements, and had diagramed where she wanted every single piece of jewelry placed on her during her viewing. The jewelry jangled as she wagged a finger at Sleepy Hollow's mayor, Anna Grace May. "I've been trying to get an appointment to see her for two weeks and she couldn't make time for me. Hmmph."

Doc Clyde had never been able to explain the touching thing. If Ruthie *was* a hallucination, how could she touch me? I rubbed my arm, trying to erase the feeling, and watched as everyone in the room turned their heads toward Mayor May.

Ruthie crossed her arms, lowered her brow and

snarled. "Must be an election year, her showing up here like this."

"She's pretty busy," I whispered.

Mayor May sashayed her way up to see old Ruthie laid out, shaking hands along the way as if she were the president of the United States about to deliver the State of the Union speech. Her long, straight auburn hair was neatly tucked behind each ear, and her tight pencil skirt showed off her curvy body in just the right places. Her perfect white teeth glistened in the dull funeral-home setting.

If she wasn't close enough to shake your hand, the mayor did her standard wink and wave. I swear that was how she got elected. Mayor May was the first Sleepy Hollow official to ever get elected to office without being born and bred here. She was a quick talker and good with the old people, who made up the majority of the population. She didn't know the history of all the familial generations—how my grandfather had built Eternal Slumber with his own hands or how Sleepy Hollow had been a big coal town back in the day—which made her a bit of an outsider. Still, she was a good mayor and everyone seemed to like her.

All the men in the room eyed Mayor May's wiggle as she made her way down the center aisle of the viewing room. A few smacks could be heard from the women punching their husbands in the arm to stop them from gawking.

Ruthie said, "I know, especially now with that new development happening in town. It's why I wanted to talk to her."

New development? This was the first time I had heard anything about a new development. There hadn't been anything new in Sleepy Hollow in . . . a long time.

We could certainly use a little developing, but it would come at the risk of disturbing Sleepy Hollow's main income. The town was a top destination in Kentucky because of our many caves and caverns. Any digging could wreak havoc with what was going on underground.

Before I could ask Ruthie for more information, she said, "It's about time *they* got here."

In the vestibule, all the blue-haired ladies from the Auxiliary Club (Ruthie's only friends) stood side by side with their pocketbooks hooked in the crooks of their elbows. They were taking their sweet time signing the guest book.

The guest book was to be given to the next of kin, whom I still hadn't had any luck finding. As a matter of fact, I didn't have any family members listed in my files for Ruthie.

Ruthie walked over to her friends, eyeing them

as they talked about her. She looked like she was chomping at the bit to join in the gossip, but put her hand up to her mouth. The corners of her eyes turned down, and a tear balanced on the edge of her eyelid as if she realized her fate had truly been sealed.

A flash of movement caught my eye, and I nearly groaned as I spotted my sister Charlotte Rae snaking through the crowd, her fiery gaze leveled on me. I tried to sidestep around Pastor Brown but was quickly jerked to a stop when she called after me.

"Did I just see you over here talking to yourself, Emma Lee?" She gave me a death stare that might just put me next to old Ruthie in her casket.

"Me? No." I laughed. When it came to Charlotte Rae, denial was my best defense.

My sister stood much taller than me. Her sparkly green eyes, long red hair, and girl-next-door look made families feel comfortable discussing their loved one's final resting needs with her. That was why she ran the sales side of our business, while I covered almost everything else.

Details. That was my specialty. I couldn't help but notice Charlotte Rae's pink nails were a perfect match to her pink blouse. She was perfectly beautiful.

Not that I was unattractive, but my brown hair

was definitely dull if I didn't get highlights, which reminded me that I needed to make an appointment at the hair salon. My hazel eyes didn't twinkle like Charlotte Rae's. Nor did my legs climb to the sky like Charlotte's. She was blessed with Grandpa Raines's family genes of long and lean, while I took after Granny's side of the family—average.

Charlotte Rae leaned over and whispered, "Seriously, are you seeing something?"

I shook my head. There was no way I was going to spill the beans about seeing Ruthie. Truth be told, I'd been positive that seeing Chicken Teater while I was in the hospital *had* been a figment of my imagination . . . until I was called to pick up Ruthie's dead body from the Sleepy Hollow Inn and Antiques, Sleepy Hollow's one and only motel.

When she started talking to me, there was no denying the truth.

I wasn't hallucinating.

I could see ghosts.

I hadn't quite figured out what to do with this newfound talent of mine, and didn't really want to discuss it with anyone until I did. Especially Charlotte. If she suspected what was going on, she'd have Doc Clyde give me one of those little pills that he said cured the "Funeral Trauma," but only made me sleepy and groggy.

Charlotte Rae leaned over and fussed at me through her gritted teeth. "If you are seeing something or *someone*, you better keep your mouth shut."

That was one thing Charlotte Rae was good at. She could keep a smile on her face and stab you in the back at the same time. She went on. "You've already lost Blue Goose Moore and Shelby Parks to Burns Funeral Home because they didn't want the 'Funeral Trauma' to rub off on them."

My lips were as tight as bark on a tree about seeing or hearing Ruthie. In fact, I didn't understand enough of it myself to speak of it.

I was saved from more denials as the Auxiliary women filed into the viewing room one by one. I jumped at the chance to make them feel welcome—and leave my sister behind. "Right this way, ladies." I gestured down the center aisle for the Auxiliary women to make their way to the casket.

One lady shook her head. "I can't believe she fell down the inn's steps. She was always so good on her feet. So sad."

"It could happen to any of us," another blue-haired lady rattled off as she consoled her friend.

"Yes, it's a sad day," I murmured and followed them up to the front of the room, stopping a few times on the way so they could say hi to some of the townsfolk they recognized.

"Fall?" Ruthie leaned against her casket as the ladies paid their respects. "What does she mean 'fall'?" Ruthie begged to know. Frantically, she looked at me and back at the lady.

I ignored her, because answering would really set town tongues to wagging, and adjusted the arrangement of roses that lay across the mahogany casket. The smell of the flowers made my stomach curl. There was a certain odor to a roomful of floral arrangements that didn't sit well with me. Even as a child, I never liked the scent.

Ruthie, however, was not going to be ignored.

"Emma Lee Raines, I know you can hear me. You listen to me." There was a desperate plea in her voice. "I didn't fall."

Okay, *that* got my attention. I needed to hear this. I gave a sharp nod of my chin, motioning for her to follow me.

Pulling my hands out of the rose arrangement, I smoothed down the front of my skirt and started to walk back down the aisle toward the entrance of the viewing room.

We'd barely made it into the vestibule before Ruthie was right in my face. "Emma Lee, I did *not* fall down those stairs. Someone pushed me. Don't you understand? I was murdered!"

A GHOSTLY GRAVE

**There's a ghost on the loose—
and a fox in the henhouse**

Four years ago, the Eternal Slumber Funeral Home put Chicken Teater in the ground. Now undertaker Emma Lee Raines is digging him back up. The whole scene is bad for business, especially with her granny running for mayor and a big festival setting up in town. But ever since Emma Lee started seeing ghosts, Chicken's been pestering her to figure out who killed him.

With her handsome boyfriend, Sheriff Jack Henry Ross, busy getting new forensics on the old corpse, Emma Lee has time to look into her first suspect. Chicken's widow may be a former Miss Kentucky, but the love of his life was another beauty queen: Lady Cluckington, his prize-winning hen. Was Mrs. Teater the jealous type? Chicken seems to think so. Something's definitely rotten in Sleepy Hollow—and Emma Lee just prays it's not her luck.

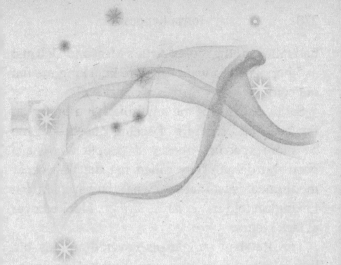

Just think, this all started because of Santa Claus. I took a drink of my large Diet Coke Big Gulp that I had picked up from the Buy and Fly gas station on the way over to Sleepy Hollow Cemetery to watch Chicken Teater's body being exhumed from his eternal resting place—only he was far from restful.

Damn Santa. I sucked up a mouthful of Diet Coke and swallowed. *Damn Santa.*

No, I didn't mean the real jolly guy with the belly shaking like a bowlful of jelly who leaves baby dolls and toy trucks; I meant the plastic light-up ornamental kind that people stick in their front yards during Christmas. The particular plastic Santa I was talking about was the one that had fallen off the roof of Artie's Meat and Deli just as I happened to walk under it, knocking me flat out cold.

Santa didn't give me anything but a bump on the head and the gift of seeing ghosts—let me be more specific—ghosts of people who have been murdered. They called me the Betweener medium, at least that was what the psychic from Lexington told us . . . *us* . . . *sigh* . . . I looked over at Jack Henry.

The Ray-Ban sunglasses covered up his big brown eyes, which were the exact same color as a Hershey's chocolate bar. I looked into his eyes. And as with a chocolate bar, once I stared at them, I was a goner. Lost, in fact.

Today I was positive his eyes would be watering from the stench of a casket that had been buried for four years—almost four years to the day, now that I thought about it.

Jack Henry, my boyfriend and Sleepy Hollow sheriff, motioned for John Howard Lloyd to drop the claw that was attached to the tractor and begin digging. John Howard, my employee at Eternal Slumber Funeral Home, didn't mind digging up the grave. He dug it four years ago, so why not? He hummed a tune, happily chewing—gumming, since he had no teeth—a piece of straw he had grabbed up off the ground before he took his post behind the tractor controls. If someone who didn't know him came upon John Howard, they'd think he was a serial killer, with his dirty overalls, wiry hair and gummy smile.

The buzz of a moped scooter caused me to look back at the street. There was a crowd that had gathered behind the yellow police line to see what was happening because it wasn't every day someone's body was plucked from its resting place.

"Zula Fae Raines Payne, get back here!" an officer scolded my granny, who didn't pay him any attention. She waved her handkerchief in the air with one hand while she steered her moped right on through the police tape. "This is a crime scene and you aren't allowed over there."

Granny didn't even wobble but held the moped steady when she snapped right through the yellow tape.

"Woo hoooo, Emma!" Granny hollered, ignoring the officer, who was getting a little too close to her. A black helmet snapped on the side covered the top of her head, giving her plenty of room to sport her large black-rimmed sunglasses. She twisted the handle to full throttle. The officer took off at a full sprint to catch up to her. He put his arm out to grab her. "I declare!" Granny jerked her head back. "I'm Zula Raines Payne, the owner of Eternal Slumber, and this is one of my clients!"

"Ma'am, I know who you are. With all due respect, because my momma and pa taught me to respect my elders—and I do respect you, Ms. Payne—I can't let you cross that tape. You are going to have to go back behind the line!" He ran behind her and pointed to the yellow tape that she had already zipped through. "This is a crime scene. Need I remind you that you turned over operations of your business to your granddaughter? And only *she* has the right to be on the other side of the line."

I curled my head back around to see what Jack Henry and John were doing and pretended the roar of the excavator was drowning out the sounds around me, including those of Granny screaming my name. Plus, I didn't want to get into any sort of argument with Granny, since half the town came out to watch the 7 a.m. exhumation, and the Auxiliary women were the first in line—and would be the first to be at the Higher Grounds Café, eating their scones, drinking their coffee and coming up with all sorts of reasons why we had exhumed the body.

I could hear them now. *Ever since Zula Fae left Emma Lee and Charlotte Rae in charge of Eternal Slumber, it's gone downhill,* or my personal favorite, *I'm not going to lay my corpse at Eternal Slumber just to have that crazy Emma Lee dig me back up. Especially since she's got a case of the Funeral Trauma.*

The "Funeral Trauma." After the whole Santa incident, I told Doc Clyde I was having some sort of hallucinations and seeing dead people. He said I had been in the funeral business a little too long and seeing corpses all of my life had been traumatic.

Regardless, the officer was half right—me and my sister were in charge of Eternal Slumber. At twenty-eight, I had been an undertaker for only three years. But, I had been around the funeral home my whole life. It is the family business, one I didn't want to do until I turned twenty-five years old and decided I better keep the business going. *Some business.* Currently, Granny still owned Eternal Slumber, but my sister, Charlotte Rae, and I ran the joint.

My parents completely retired and moved to Florida. Thank God for Skype or I'd never see them. I guess Granny was semi-retired. I say semi-retired because she put her two cents in when she wanted to. Today she wanted to.

Some family business.

Granny brought the moped to an abrupt stop. She hopped right off and flicked the snap of the strap and pulled the helmet off along with her sunglasses. She hung the helmet on the handle-bars and the glasses dangled from the *V* in her sweater exactly where she wanted it to hang—between her boobs. Doc Clyde was there and Granny had him on the hook exactly where she wanted to keep him.

Her short flaming-red hair looked like it was on fire, with the morning sun beaming down as she used her fingers to spike it up a little more than usual. After all, she knew she had to look good because she was the center of attention—next to Chicken Teater's exhumed body.

The officer ran up and grabbed the scooter's handle. He knew better than to touch Granny.

"I am sure your momma and pa did bring you up right, but if you don't let me go . . ." Granny jerked the scooter toward her. She was a true Southern belle and put things in a way that no other woman could. I looked back at them and waved her over. The police officer stepped aside. Granny took her hanky out of her bra and wiped off the officer's shoulder like she was cleaning lint or something. "It was *lovely* to meet you." Granny's voice dripped like sweet honey. She put the hanky back where she had gotten it.

I snickered. *Lovely* wasn't always a compliment from a Southern gal. Like the gentleman he claimed to be, he took his hat off to Granny and smiled.

She didn't pay him any attention as she bee-lined it toward me.

"Hi," she said in her sweet Southern drawl, waving at everyone around us. She gave a little extra wink toward Doc Clyde. His cheeks rose to a scarlet red. Nervously, he ran his fingers through his thinning hair and pushed it to the side, defining the side part.

Everyone in town knew he had been keeping late hours just for Granny, even though she wasn't a bit sick. God knew what they were doing and I didn't want to know.

Granny pointed her hanky toward Pastor Brown who was there to say a little prayer when the casket was exhumed. Waking the dead wasn't high on anyone's priority list. Granny put the cloth over her mouth and leaning in, she whispered, "Emma Lee, you better have a good reason to be digging up Chicken Teater."

We both looked at the large concrete chicken gravestone. The small gold plate at the base of the stone statue displayed all of Colonel Chicken Teater's stats with his parting words: *Chicken has left the coop.*

"Why don't you go worry about the Inn." I suggested for her to leave and glanced over at John Howard. He had to be getting close to reaching the casket vault.

Granny gave me the stink-eye.

"It was only a suggestion." I put my hands up in the air as a truce sign.

Granny owned, operated and lived at the only bed-and-breakfast in town, the Sleepy Hollow Inn, known as "the Inn" around here. Everyone loved staying at the large mansion, which sat at the foothills of the caverns and caves that made Sleepy Hollow a main attraction in Kentucky . . . besides horses and University of Kentucky basketball.

Sleepy Hollow was a small tourist town that was low on crime, and that was the way we liked it.

Sniff, sniff. Whimpers were coming from underneath the large black floppy hat.

Granny and I looked over at Marla Maria Teater, Chicken's wife. She had come dressed to the nines with her black V-neck dress hitting her curves in all the right places. The hat covered up the eyes she was dabbing.

Of course, when the police notified her that they had good reason to believe that Chicken didn't die of a serious bout of pneumonia but was murdered, Marla took to her bed as any mourning widow would. She insisted on being here for the exhumation. Jack Henry had warned Marla Maria to keep quiet about why the police were opening up the files on Chicken's death. If there was a murderer on the loose and it got around, it could possibly hurt the economy, and this was Sleepy Hollow's busiest time of the year.

Granny put her arm around Marla and winked at me over Marla's shoulder.

"Now, now. I know it's hard, honey, I've buried a few myself. Granted, I've never had any dug up though." Granny wasn't lying. She has been twice widowed and I was hoping she'd stay away from marriage a third time. Poor Doc Clyde, you'd have thought he would stay away from her since her track record was . . . well . . . deadly. "That's a first in this town." Granny gave Marla Maria the elbow along with a wink and a click of her tongue.

Maybe the third time was the charm.

"Who is buried here?" Granny let go of Marla and stepped over to the smaller tombstone next to Chicken's.

"Stop!" Jack Henry screamed, waving his hands in the air. "Zula, move!"

Granny looked up and ducked just as John Howard came back for another bite of ground with the claw.

I would hate to have to bury Granny anytime soon.

"Lady Cluckington," Marla whispered, tilting

her head to the side. Using her finger, she dabbed the driest eyes I had ever seen. "Our prize chicken. Well, she isn't dead *yet*."

I glanced over at her. Her tone caused a little suspicion to stir in my gut.

"She's not a chicken. She's a Spangled Russian Orloff Hen!" Chicken Teater appeared next to his grave. His stone looked small next to his six-foot-two frame. He ran his hand over the tombstone Granny had asked about. There was a date of birth, but no date of death. "You couldn't stand having another beauty queen in my life!"

"Oh no," I groaned and took another gulp of my Diet Coke. He—his ghost—was the last thing that I needed to see this morning.

"Is that sweet tea?" Chicken licked his lips. "I'd give anything to have a big ole sip of sweet tea." He towered over me. His hair was neatly combed to the right; his red plaid shirt was tucked into his carpenter jeans.

This was the third time I had seen Chicken Teater since his death. It was a shock to the community to hear of a man passing from pneumonia in his early sixties. But that was what the doctors in Lexington said he died of, no questions asked, and his funeral was held at Eternal Slumber.

The first time I had seen Chicken Teater's ghost

was after my perilous run-in with Santa. I too thought I was a goner, gone to the great beyond . . . but no . . . Chicken Teater and Ruthie Sue Payne—their ghosts anyway—stood right next to my hospital bed, eyeballing me. Giving me the onceover as if he was trying to figure out if I was dead or alive. Lucky for him I was alive and seeing him.

Ruthie Sue Payne was a client at Eternal Slumber who couldn't cross over until someone helped her solve her murder. That someone was me. The Betweener.

Since I could see her, talk to her, feel her and hear her, I was the one. Thanks to me, Ruthie's murder was solved and she was now resting peacefully on the other side. Chicken was a different story.

Apparently, Ruthie was as big of a gossip in the afterlife as she was in her earthly life. That was how Chicken Teater knew about me being a Betweener. Evidently, Ruthie was telling everyone about my special gift.

Chicken Teater wouldn't leave me alone until I agreed to investigate his death because he knew he didn't die from pneumonia. He claimed he was poisoned. But who would want to kill a chicken farmer?

Regardless, it took several months of me trying to convince Jack Henry there might be a possibility Chicken Teater was murdered. After some questionable evidence, provided by Chicken Teater, the case was reopened. I didn't understand all the red tape and legal yip-yap, but here we stood today.

Now it was time for me to get Chicken Teater to the other side.

"It's not dead yet?" Granny's eyebrows rose in amazement after Marla Maria confirmed there was an empty grave. Granny couldn't get past the fact there was a gravestone for something that wasn't dead.

I was still stuck on "prize chicken." What was a prize chicken?

A loud thud echoed when John Howard sent the claw down. There was an audible gasp from the crowd. The air was thick with anticipation. What did they think they were going to see?

Suddenly my nerves took a downward dive. What if the coffin opened? Coffin makers guaranteed they lock for eternity after they are sealed, but still, it wouldn't be a good thing for John Howard to pull the coffin up and have Chicken take a tumble next to Lady Cluckington's stone.

"I think we got 'er!" John Howard stood up in the cab of the digger with pride on his face as he looked down in the hole. "Yep! That's it!" he hollered over the roar of the running motor.

Jack Henry ran over and hooked some cables on the excavator and gave the thumbs-up.

Pastor Brown dipped his head and moved his lips in a silent prayer. Granny nudged me with her boney elbow to bow my head, and I did. Marla Maria cried out.

"Aw shut up!" Chicken Teater told her and smiled as he saw his coffin being raised from the earth. "They are going to figure out who killed me, and so help me, if it was you . . ." He shook his fist in the air in Marla Maria's direction.

Curiosity stirred in my bones. Was it going to be easy getting Chicken Teater to the other side? Was Marla Maria Teater behind his death as Chicken believed?

She was the only one who was not only in his bed at night, but right by his deathbed, so he told me. I took my little notebook out from my back pocket. I had learned from Ruthie's investigation to never leave home without it. I jotted down what Chicken had said to Marla Maria, with prize chickens next to it, followed up by a lot of exclamation points. Oh . . . I had almost forgotten that Marla Maria was Miss Kentucky in her earlier years—a *beauty queen*—I quickly wrote that down too.

"Are you getting all of this?" Chicken questioned me and twirled his finger in a circle as he

referred to the little scene Marla Maria was causing with her meltdown. She leaned her butt up
against Lady Cluckington's stone. Chicken rushed
over to his prize chicken's gravestone and tried to
shove Marla Maria off. "Get your—"

Marla Maria jerked like she could feel something touch her. She shivered. Her body shimmied from her head to her toes.

I cleared my throat, doing my best to get
Chicken to stop fusing and cursing. "Are you
okay?" I asked. Did she feel him?

Granny stood there taking it all in.

Marla crossed her arms in front of her and ran
her hands up and down them. "I guess when I
buried Chicken, I thought that was the end of it.
This is creeping me out a little bit."

End of it? End of what? Your little murder plot? My
mind unleashed all sorts of ways Marla Maria
might have offed her man. That seemed a little too
suspicious for me. Marla buttoned her lip when
Jack Henry walked over. More suspicious behavior that I duly noted.

"Can you tell me how he died?" I put a hand on
her back to offer some comfort, though I knew she
was putting on a good act.

She shook her head, dabbed her eye and said,
"He was so sick. Coughing and hacking. I was so

mad because I had bags under my eyes from him keeping me up at night." *Sniff, sniff.* "I had to dab some Preparation H underneath my eyes in order to shrink them." She tapped her face right above her cheekbones.

"That's where my butt cream went?" Chicken hooted and hollered. "She knew I had a hemorrhoid the size of a golf ball and she used my cream on her face?" Chicken flailed his arms around in the air.

I bit my lip and stepped a bit closer to Marla Maria so I couldn't see Chicken out of my peripheral vision. There were a lot of things I had heard in my time, but hemorrhoids were something that I didn't care to know about.

I stared at Marla Maria's face. There wasn't a tear, a tear streak, or a single wrinkle on her perfectly made-up face. If hemorrhoids helped shrink her under-eye bags, did it also help shrink her wrinkles?

"Anyway, enough about me." She fanned her face with the handkerchief. "Chicken was so uncomfortable with all the phlegm. He could barely breathe. I let him rest, but called the doctor in the meantime." She nodded and waited for me to agree with her. I nodded back and she continued. "When the doctor came out of the bedroom, he told me Chicken was dead." A cry burst out of her as she threw her head back and held the hanky over her face.

I was sure she was hiding a smile from thinking she was pulling one over on me. Little did she know this wasn't my first rodeo with a murderer. Still, I patted her back while Chicken spat at her feet.

Jack Henry walked over. He didn't take his eyes off of Marla Maria.

"I'm sorry we have to do this, Marla." Jack took his hat off out of respect for the widow. *Black widow,* I thought as I watched her fidget side to side, avoiding all eye contact by dabbing the corners of her eyes. "We are all done here, Zula." He nodded toward Granny.

Granny smiled.

Marla Maria nodded before she turned to go face her waiting public behind the police line.

Granny walked over to say something to Doc Clyde, giving him a little butt pat and making his face even redder than before. I waited until she was out of earshot before I said something to Jack Henry.

"That was weird. Marla Maria is a good actress." I made mention to Jack Henry because sometimes he was clueless as to how women react to different situations.

"Don't be going and blaming her just because she's his wife." Jack Henry was trying to play the good cop he always was, but I wasn't falling for his act. "It's all speculation at this point."

"Wife? She was no kind of wife to me." Chicken kicked his foot in the dirt John Howard had dug from his grave. "She only did one thing as my wife." Chicken looked back and watched Marla Maria play the poor pitiful widow as Beulah Paige Bellefry, president and CEO of Sleepy Hollow's gossip mill, drew her into a big hug while all the other Auxiliary women gathered to put in their two cents.

"La-la-la." I put my fingers in my ears and tried to drown him out. I only wanted to know how he was murdered, not how Marla Maria *was* a wife to him.

"She spent all my money," he cursed under his breath.

"*Shoo.*" I let out an audible sigh.

Over Jack's right shoulder, in the distance some movement caught my eye near the trailer park. There was a man peering out from behind a tree looking over at all the commotion. His John Deere hat helped shadow his face so I couldn't get a good look, but I chalked it up to being a curious neighbor like the rest of them. Still, I quickly wrote down the odd behavior. I had learned you never know what people knew. And I had to start from scratch on how to get Chicken to the great beyond. I wasn't sure, but I believe Chicken had lived in the trailer park. Maybe the person saw something, maybe not. He was going on the list.

"Are you okay?" Jack pulled off his sunglasses. His big brown eyes were set with worry. I grinned. A smile ruffled his mouth. "Just checking because of the la-la thing." He waved his hands in the air. "I saw you taking some notes and I know what that means."

"Yep." My one word confirmed that Chicken was there and spewing all sorts of valuable information. Jack Henry was the only person who knew I was a Betweener, and he knew Chicken was right here with us even though he couldn't see him. When I told him about Chicken Teater's little visits to me and how he wouldn't leave me alone until we figured out who killed him, Jack Henry knew it to be true. "I'll tell you later."

I jotted down a note about Marla Maria spending all of Chicken's money, or so he said. Which made me question her involvement even more. Was he no use to her with a zero bank account and she offed him? I didn't know he had money.

"I can see your little noggin running a mile a minute." Jack bent down and looked at me square in the eyes.

"Just taking it all in." I bit my lip. I had learned from my last ghost that I had to keep some things to myself until I got the full scoop. And right now, Chicken hadn't given me any solid information.

"You worry about getting all the information you can from your little friend." Jack Henry pointed to the air beside me. I pointed to the air beside him where Chicken's ghost was actually standing. Jack grimaced. "Whatever. I don't care where he is." He shivered.

Even though Jack Henry knew I could see ghosts, he wasn't completely comfortable.

"You leave the investigation to me." Jack Henry put his sunglasses back on. Sexy dripped from him, making my heart jump a few beats.

"Uh-huh." I looked away. Looking away from Jack Henry when he was warning me was a common occurrence. I knew I had to do my own investigating and couldn't get lost in his eyes while lying to him.

Besides, I didn't have a whole lot of information. Chicken knew he was murdered but had no clue how. He was only able to give me clues about his life and it was up to me to put them together.

"I'm not kidding." Jack Henry took his finger and put it on my chin, pulling it toward him. He gave me a quick kiss. "We are almost finished up here. I'll sign all the paperwork and send the body on over to Eternal Slumber for Vernon to get going on some new toxicology reports we have ordered." He took his officer hat off and used his forearm to wipe the sweat off his brow.

"He's there waiting," I said. Vernon Baxter was a retired doctor who performed any and all autopsies the Sleepy Hollow police needed and I let him use Eternal Slumber for free. I had all the newest technology and equipment used in autopsies in the basement of the funeral home.

"Go on up!" Jack Henry gave John the thumbs-up and walked closer. Slowly John Howard lifted the coffin completely out of the grave and sat it right on top of the church truck, which looked like a gurney.

"Do you think she did it?" I glanced over at Marla Maria, as she talked a good talk.

"Did what?" Granny walked up and asked. She turned to see what I was looking at. "Did you dig him up because his death is being investigated for murder?" Granny gasped.

"Now Granny, don't go spreading rumors." I couldn't deny or admit to what she said. If I admitted the truth to her question, I would be betraying Jack Henry. If I denied her question, I would be lying to Granny. And no one lies to Granny.

In a lickety-split, Granny was next to her scooter.

"I'll be over. Put the coffee on," Granny hollered before she put her helmet back on her head, snapped the strap in place, and revved up the scooter and buzzed off in the direction of town, giving a little *toot-toot* and wave to the Auxiliary women as she passed.

Once the chains were unhooked from the coffin and the excavator was out of the way, Jack Henry and I guided the coffin on the church truck into the back of my hearse. Before I shut the door, I had a sick feeling that someone was watching me. Of course the crowd was still there, but I mean someone was watching *my* every move.

I looked back over my shoulder toward the trailer park. The man in the John Deere hat popped out of sight behind the tree when he saw me look at him.

I shut the hearse door and got into the driver's side. Before I left the cemetery, I looked in my rearview mirror at the tree. The man was standing there. This time the shadow of the hat didn't hide his eyes.

We locked eyes.

"Look away," Chicken Teater warned me when he appeared in the passenger seat.

A GHOSTLY DEMISE

**The prodigal father returns—
but this ghost is no holy spirit**

When she runs into her friend's deadbeat dad at the local deli, undertaker Emma Lee Raines can't wait to tell Mary Anna Hardy that he's back in Sleepy Hollow, Kentucky, after five long years. Cephus Hardy may have been the town drunk, but he didn't disappear on an epic bender like everyone thought: He was murdered. And he's heard that Emma Lee's been helping lost souls move on to that great big party in the sky.

Why do ghosts always bother Emma Lee at the worst times? Her granny's mayoral campaign is in high gear, a carnival is taking over the Town Square, and her hunky boyfriend, Sheriff Jack Henry Ross, is stuck wrestling runaway goats. Besides, Cephus has no clue whodunit . . . unless it was one of Mrs. Hardy's not-so-secret admirers. All roads lead Emma Lee to that carnival—and a killer who isn't clowning around.

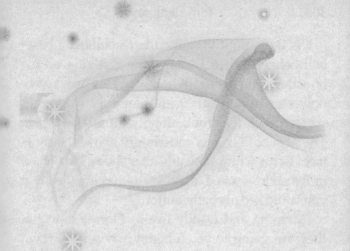

"Cephus Hardy?"

Stunned. My jaw dropped when I saw Cephus Hardy walk up to me in the magazine aisle of Artie's Meat and Deli. I was admiring the cover of *Cock and Feathers*, where my last client at Eternal Slumber Funeral Home, Chicken Teater, graced the cover with his prize Orloff Hen, Lady Cluckington.

"I declare." A Mack truck could've hit me and I wouldn't have felt it. I grinned from ear to ear.

Cephus Hardy looked the exact same as he did five years ago. Well, from what I could remember from his social visits with my momma and daddy and the few times I had seen him around our small town of Sleepy Hollow, Kentucky.

His tight, light brown curls resembled a baseball helmet. When I was younger, it amazed me how thick and dense his hair was. He always wore polyester taupe pants with the perfectly straight crease down the front, along with a brown belt. The hem of his pants ended right above the shoelaces in his white, patent-leather shoes. He tucked in his short-sleeved, plaid shirt, making it so taut you could see his belly button.

"Momma and Daddy live in Florida now, but they are going to be so happy when I tell them you are back in town. Everyone has been so worried about you." I smiled and took in his sharp, pointy nose and rosy red cheeks. I didn't take my eyes off him as I put the copy of *Cock and Feathers* back in the rack. I leaned on my full cart of groceries and noticed he hadn't even aged a bit. No wrinkles. Nothing. "Where the hell have you been?"

He shrugged. He rubbed the back of his neck.

"Who cares?" I really couldn't believe it. Mary Anna was going to be so happy since he had just up and left five years ago, telling no one—nor had he contacted anyone since. "You won't believe what Granny is doing."

I pointed over his shoulder at the election poster taped up on Artie's Meat and Deli's storefront window.

"Granny is running against O'Dell Burns for mayor." I cackled, looking in the distance at the poster of Zula Fae Raines Payne all laid-back in the rocking chair on the front porch of the Sleepy Hollow Inn with a glass of her famous iced tea in her hand.

It took us ten times to get a picture she said was good enough to use on all her promotional items for the campaign. Since she was all of five-foot-four, her feet dangled. She didn't want people to vote on her size; therefore, the photo was from the lap up. I told Granny that I didn't know who she thought she was fooling. Everyone who was eligible to vote knew her and how tall she was. She insisted. I didn't argue anymore. No one, and I mean no one, wins an argument against Zula Fae Raines Payne. Including me.

"She looks good." Cephus raised his brows, lips turned down.

"She sure does," I noted.

For a twice-widowed seventy-seven-year-old, Granny acted like she was in her fifties. I wasn't sure if her red hair was still hers or if Mary Anna kept it up on the down-low, but Granny would never be seen going to Girl's Best Friend unless there was some sort of gossip that needed to be heard. Otherwise, she wanted everyone to see her as the good Southern belle she was.

"Against O'Dell Burns?" Cephus asked. Slowly, he nodded in approval.

It was no secret that Granny and O'Dell had butted heads a time or two. The outcome of the election was going to be interesting, to say the least.

"Yep. She retired three years ago, leaving me and Charlotte Rae in charge of Eternal Slumber."

It was true. I was the undertaker of Eternal Slumber Funeral Home. It might make some folks' skin crawl to think about being around dead people all the time, but it was job security at its finest. O'Dell Burns owned Burns Funeral, the other funeral home in Sleepy Hollow, which made him and Granny enemies from the get-go.

O'Dell didn't bother me though. Granny didn't see it that way. We needed a new mayor, and O'Dell stepped up to the plate at the council meeting, but Granny wouldn't hear of it. So the competition didn't stop with dead people; now Granny wants all the living people too. As mayor.

"Long story short," I rambled on and on, "Granny married Earl Way Payne. He died and left Granny the Sleepy Hollow Inn. I don't know what she is thinking running for mayor because she's so busy taking care of all of the tourists at the Inn. Which reminds me"—I planted my hands on my hips—"you never answered my question. Have you seen Mary Anna yet?"

"Not yet." His lips curved in a smile.

"She's done real good for herself. She opened Girl's Best Friend Spa and has all the business since she's the only one in town. And"—I wiggled my brows—"she is working for me at Eternal Slumber."

A shiver crawled up my spine and I did a little shimmy shake, thinking about her fixing the corpses' hair and makeup. Somebody had to do it and Mary Anna didn't seem to mind a bit.

I ran my hand down my brown hair that Mary Anna had recently dyed since my short stint as a blond. I couldn't do my own hair, much less someone else's. Same for the makeup department.

I never spent much time in front of the mirror. I worked with the dead and they weren't judging me.

"Emma Lee?" Doc Clyde stood at the end of the magazine aisle with a small shopping basket in the crook of his arm. His lips set in a tight line. "Are you feeling all right?"

"Better than ever." My voice rose when I pointed to Cephus. "Especially now that Cephus is back in town."

"Have you been taking your meds for the Funeral Trauma?" He ran his free hand in his thin hair, placing the few remaining strands to the side. His chin was pointy and jutted out even more as he shuffled his thick-soled doctor shoes down the old, tiled floor. "You know, it's only been nine months since your accident. And it could take years before the symptoms go away."

"Funeral Trauma," I muttered, and rolled my eyes.

Cephus just grinned.

The Funeral Trauma.

A few months back I had a perilous incident with a plastic Santa Claus right here at Artie's Meat and Deli. I had walked down from the funeral home to grab some lunch. Artie had thought it was a good idea to put a life-sized plastic Santa on the roof. It was a good idea until the snow started melting and the damn thing slid right off the roof just as I was walking by, knocking me square out. Flat.

I woke up in the hospital seeing ghosts of the corpse I had buried six feet deep. I thought I had gone to the Great Beyond. But I could see my family and all the living.

I told Doc Clyde I was having some sort of hallucinations and seeing dead people. He said I had been in the funeral business a little too long and seeing corpses all of my life had been traumatizing. Granny had been in the business for over forty years. I had only been in the business for three. Something didn't add up.

Turned out, a psychic confirmed I am what was called a Betweener.

I could see ghosts of the dead who were stuck between the here and the after. Of course, no one but me and Jack Henry, my boyfriend and Sleepy Hollow's sheriff, knew. And he was still a little apprehensive about the whole thing.

"I'm fine," I assured Doc Clyde, and looked at Cephus. "Wait." I stopped and tried to swallow what felt like a mound of sand in my mouth. My mind hit rewind and took me back to the beginning of my conversation with Cephus.

A GHOSTLY MURDER

**Emma Lee Raines knows there's only
one cure for a bad case of murder**

I told you I was sick, reads the headstone above
Mamie Sue Preston's grave. She was the richest
woman in Sleepy Hollow, Kentucky, and also the
biggest hypochondriac. Ironic, considering someone killed her—and covered it up perfectly. And
how does Emma Lee, proprietor of the Eternal
Slumber Funeral Home, know all this? Because
Mamie Sue's host told her, that's how. And she's
offering big bucks to find the perp.

The catch is, Mamie Sue was buried by the
Raines family's archrival, Burns Funeral Home.
Would the Burnses stoop to framing Emma Lee's
granny? With an enterprising maid, a penny-
pinching pastor and a slimy Lexington lawyer all
making a killing off Mamie Sue's estate, Emma
Lee needs a teammate—like her dreamboat boyfriend, Sheriff Jack Henry Ross. Because with mil-
lions at stake, snooping around is definitely bad
for Emma Lee's health.

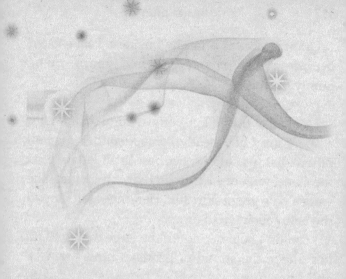

Ding, ding, ding.

The ornamental bell on an old cemetery headstone rang out. No one touching it. No wind or breeze.

The string attached to the top of the bell hung down the stone and disappeared into the ground. To the naked eye it would seem as though the bell dinged from natural causes, like the wind, but my eye zeroed in on the string as it slowly moved up and down. Deliberately.

I stepped back and looked at the stone. The chiseled words I TOLD YOU I WAS SICK. MAMIE SUE PRESTON were scrolled in fancy lettering. Her date of death was a few years before I took over as undertaker at Eternal Slumber Funeral Home.

Granted, it was a family business I had taken over from my parents and my granny. Some family business.

Ding, ding, ding.

I looked at the bell. A petite older woman, with a short gray bob neatly combed under a small pillbox hat, was doing her best to sit ladylike on the stone, with one leg crossed over the other. She wore a pale green skirt suit. Her fingernail tapped the bell, causing it to ding.

I couldn't help but notice the large diamond on her finger, the strand of pearls around her neck and some more wrapped on her wrist. And with a gravestone like that . . . I knew she came from money.

"Honey child, you can see me, can't you?" she asked. Her lips smacked together. She grinned, not a tooth in her head. There was a cane in her hand. She tapped the stone with it. "Can you believe they buried me without my teeth?"

I closed my eyes. Squeezed them tight. Opened them back up.

"Ta-da. Still here." She put the cane on the ground and tap-danced around it on her own grave.

"Don't do that. It's bad luck." I repeated another Southern phrase I had heard all my life.

She did another little giddy-up.

"I'm serious," I said in a flat, inflectionless voice. "Never dance or walk over someone's grave. It's bad luck."

"Honey, my luck couldn't get any worse than it already is." Her face was drawn. Her onyx eyes set. Her jaw tensed. "Thank Gawd you are here. There is no way I can cross over without my teeth." She smacked her lips. "Oh, by the way, Digger Spears just sent me, and I passed Cephus Hardy on the way. He told me exactly where I could find you."

She leaned up against the stone.

"Let me introduce myself." She stuck the cane in the crook of her elbow and adjusted the pillbox hat on her head. "I'm the wealthiest woman in Sleepy Hollow, Mamie Sue Preston, and I can pay you whatever you'd like to get me to the other side. But first, can you find my teeth?"

I tried to swallow the lump in my throat. This couldn't be happening. Couldn't I have just a few days off between my Betweener clients?

I knew exactly what she meant when she said she needed my help for her cross over, and it wasn't because she was missing her dentures.

"Whatdaya say?" Mamie Sue pulled some cash out of her suit pocket.

She licked her finger and peeled each bill back one at a time.

"Emma Lee," I heard someone call. I turned to see Granny waving a handkerchief in the air and bolting across the cemetery toward me.

Her flaming-red hair darted about like a cardinal as she weaved in and out of the gravestones.

"See," I muttered under my breath and made sure my lips didn't move. "Granny knows not to step on a grave."

"That's about the only thing Zula Fae Raines Payne knows," Mamie said.

My head whipped around. Mamie's words got my attention. Amusement lurked in her dark eyes.

"Everyone is wondering what you are doing clear over here when you are overseeing Cephus Hardy's funeral way over there." Granny took a swig of the can of Stroh's she was holding.

Though our small town of Sleepy Hollow, Kentucky, was a dry county—which meant liquor sales were against the law—I had gotten special permission to have a beer toast at Cephus Hardy's funeral.

I glanced back at the final resting place where everyone from Cephus's funeral was still sitting under the burial awning, sipping on the beer.

"I was just looking at this old stone," I lied.

Mamie's lips pursed suspiciously when she looked at Granny. Next thing I knew, Mamie was sitting on her stone, legs crossed, tapping the bell.

Ding, ding, ding. "We have a goner who needs help!" Mamie continued to ding the bell. "A goner who is as dead as yesterday." She twirled her cane around her finger.

I did my best to ignore her. If Granny knew I was able to see the ghosts of dead people—not just any dead people, murdered dead people—she'd have me committed for what Doc Clyde called the Funeral Trauma.

A few months ago and a couple ghosts ago, I was knocked out cold from a big plastic Santa that Artie, from Artie's Meat and Deli, had stuck on the roof of his shop during the winter months. It just so happened I was walking on the sidewalk when the sun melted the snow away, sending the big fella off the roof right on top of me. I woke up in the hospital and saw that my visitor was one of my clients—one of my *dead* clients. I thought I was a goner just like him, because my Eternal Slumber clients weren't alive, they were dead, and here was one standing next to me.

When the harsh realization came to me that I wasn't dead and I was able to see dead people, I told Doc Clyde about it. He gave me some little pills and diagnosed me with the Funeral Trauma, a.k.a. a case of the crazies.

He was nice enough to say he thought I had been around dead bodies too long since I had grown up in the funeral home with Granny and my parents.

My parents took early retirement and moved to Florida, while my granny also retired, leaving me and my sister, Charlotte Rae, in charge.

"Well?" Granny tapped her toe and crossed her arms. "Are you coming back to finish the funeral or not?" She gave me the stink-eye, along with a once-over, before she slung back the can and finished off the beer. "Are you feeling all right?"

"I'm feeling great, Zula Fae Raines Payne." Mamie Sue leaned her cane up against her stone. She jumped down and clasped her hands in front of her. She stretched them over her head. She jostled her head side to side. "Much better now that I can move about, thanks to Emma Lee."

Ahem, I cleared my throat.

"Yes." I smiled and passed Granny on the way back over to Cephus Hardy's funeral. "I'm on my way."

"Wait!" Mamie called out. "I was murdered! Aren't you going to help me? Everyone said that you were the one to help me!"

Everyone? I groaned and glanced back.

Mamie Sue Preston planted her hands on her small hips. Her eyes narrowed. Her bubbly personality had dimmed. She'd been dead a long time. She wasn't going anywhere anytime soon, and neither was I.

A GHOSTLY REUNION

That ghost sure looks . . . familiar

Proprietor of the Eternal Slumber Funeral Home, Emma Lee can see, hear and talk to ghosts of murdered folks. And when her high school nemesis is found dead, Jade Lee Peel is the same old mean girl—trying to come between Emma Lee and her hot boyfriend, Sheriff Jack Henry Ross, all over again.

There's only one way for Emma Lee to be free of the trash-talking ghost—solve the murder so the former prom queen can cross over.

But the last thing Jade Lee wants is to leave the town where she had her glory days. And the more Emma Lee investigates on her own, the more complicated Miss Popularity turns out to be. Now Emma Lee will have to work extra closely with her hunky lawman to get to the twisty truth.

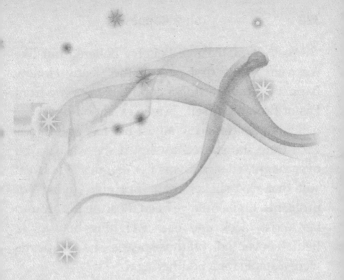

Sexy isn't a firm fanny in a thong, ladies." Hettie Bell didn't seem so sexy in her hot pink leggings and matching top as she gasped for breath in her downward dog position in the middle of Sleepy Hollow, Kentucky. Her butt stuck straight up in the air, right there on display for everyone to see. Her black, chin-length bob was falling out of the small ponytail on both sides and her bangs hung down in her eyes. "Sexy is confidence and self-acceptance. It's exactly what yoga provides."

Hettie Bell curled up on her tiptoes with her palms planted on one of the mats she provided for us. The rickety old floor of the gazebo, in the middle of the town square, groaned as we all tried to mimic her pose.

"Yes!" Beulah Paige Bellefry hollered out like we were in the first pew of the Sleepy Hollow Baptist Church getting a good Bible beating from Pastor Brown himself. "Amen to a good pose!"

Beulah continued to adjust her feet and hands each time she started to slip. If she wasn't a bit overweight, I'd say it was her eighties silk sweat suit that was slicker than cat's guts giving her problems. Or it could've been those pearls around her wrist, neck and ears weighing her down. Beulah never took off those pearls. She said pearls were a staple for a Southern gal.

"You said it, sister," Mary Anna Hardy gasped. She teetered side to side, nearly knocking into Granny. Her sweat left streaks down her makeup. Who on earth got up this early and put makeup on to do yoga? Mary Anna Hardy, that's who. "God help us!"

"That's it." I pushed back off my heels and crossed my legs staring at all the Auxiliary women's derrieres at my eye level. "I'm here to do some relaxing, not Sunday school."

Sleepy Hollow was smack-dab in the middle of the Bible Belt and if God wasn't thrown in our conversations, then we weren't breathing. But the last thing I wanted to think about was my butt stuck up to the high heavens and everyone up in the Great Beyond looking down upon me.

Trust me, not a sight the living want to see at eight o'clock in the morning, either. Especially when I hadn't had my first cup of coffee for the day.

"Emma Lee Raines," Zula Fae Raines Payne, also known as my granny, gasped in horror. "Where are your Southern manners?" Granny's disgust of my behavior was written all over her contorted face.

My redheaded Granny only stood five-foot-four, but she was a mighty force to be reckoned with. At the ripe young age of seventy-seven, she'd give you the business while blessing your heart and pouring you a glass of her sweet iced tea no matter how mad you made her.

"My manners are right over there at Higher Grounds Café in liquid form in a large foam cup." I pushed back a strand of my brown hair that had fallen out of the topknot I stuck it in after I'd rolled out of bed when I decided to join the Auxiliary women and Hettie Bell for their morning yoga class. I needed my caffeine fix to wake my manners up.

"This reunion has helped you misplace them." Granny's disapproval of how I was handling the stress of planning my ten-year high school reunion showed in the creases around her tight lips, cocked brows and furled nose. "Doc said you need to take the necessary precautions to keep the 'Trauma' away, especially in times of extreme stress."

What did Doc Clyde know? Nothing.

"I'm sure you are stressed with no one to bury around here." Granny did a sign of the cross and we weren't even Catholic. She snapped her finger at me. "Now, downward dog, young lady," she ordered.

Doc Clyde, Sleepy Hollow's resident doctor, felt it necessary I do some type of stress relief since he had diagnosed me with what he called "Funeral Trauma" after I had gotten knocked out flat cold from a falling plastic Santa and woke up in the hospital seeing the clients I had stuck six feet in the ground. Being an undertaker can be stressful, but I didn't have "Funeral Trauma." I was a Betweener.

I saw dead people. Let me clarify, dead people that had been murdered. It was a gift that plastic Santa gave me. Unlike the annual ugly Christmas sweater Granny gave me, it was a gift that I can't return. Honestly, I wouldn't even be able to take the sweater back.

"It's okay, Zula Fae." Hettie Bell dipped back down into the stretch that started all this downward dog stuff. "Yoga isn't for everyone."

"You got that right," I grumbled under my breath and watched with a dutiful eye as the white convertible Mercedes whipped into a parking spot right in front of Higher Grounds.

Sleepy Hollow was a tourist town in Kentucky. We were known for our caves and caverns. Tourists to our town were mainly the outdoorsy type that loved to spelunk and stuff that I wasn't interested in doing. Now yoga was added to that list as well.

"Uh-un!" A woman jumped out of the convertible and wagged her hand at the car trying to park in the space behind her.

The woman had on a pair of big black sunglasses that took up nearly all of her thin face and a black scarf over her hair and tied under her chin. She wore a black strapless jumpsuit and her legs looked a mile long.

"Move!" she screamed at a car that was less desirable than hers. "You aren't parking that beater behind mine!"

She jumped into her car and backed it up, taking up the only two available spaces in front of the café.

"Is that?" Beulah Paige jumped up, tugged on the hem of her silky zip top and squinted.

"You know your fancy wrinkle cream might work if you got you some glasses or contact lenses." Mable Claire cackled and jingled all the way down to her mat.

"Oh, hush, Mable Claire," Beulah warned, keeping her eyes on the little scuffle going on in front of the café. "I do think that is . . ."

Beulah ran her hand over her bright red hair, pushing her fingertips in and fluffing it up. She put her hands on the strand of pearls around her neck and straightened them.

"Oh my God." Shock and awe came over me. Then anger when I saw who it was.

Jade Lee Peel.

I stood up to steady my shaking body. It took everything in my power not to throw one big hissy fit right there in front of all of Sleepy Hollow or at least the Auxiliary women.

"It is!" Beulah jumped up and clapped her hands together like a little schoolgirl, not the forty-something-year-old gossip queen I was used to seeing.

Beulah did a little two-step and giddyup down the steps of the gazebo and scurried across the town square.

"And it looks like Jack Henry is happy to see whoever that is too." Granny sure didn't know when or how to keep her mouth shut. Especially in an emergency such as this.

"Jade Lee Peel," I grumbled and gave my high school arch-nemesis the evil eye.

It was a time like this I wished I had some sort

of cool gift like casting spells on people, not seeing them after the spell took effect and stopped their beating heart.

Jade Lee had left Sleepy Hollow right out of high school to pursue a modeling career. When she made it on a music channel's reality TV show where they all lived in a house, she was discovered. She wasn't the biggest star on the planet, but she was the biggest from Sleepy Hollow.

Reluctantly I had sent her people an invitation to the class reunion hoping they'd think it was fan mail and when I hadn't gotten back an RSVP, I'd assumed she wasn't coming. It would be just like her not to RSVP and then make a grand entrance.

"I take it you aren't so happy to see her?" Hettie stood next to me with her hands on her hips and her leg cocked to the side.

Hettie Bell was lucky and didn't know just how evil Jade Lee Peel was as a teenager. Hettie had recently moved to Sleepy Hollow and opened up Pose and Relax yoga studio next to Eternal Slumber. She would've definitely been one of Jade's targets with her Goth girl look. Mary Anna Hardy down at Girl's Best Friend Spa tee-totally gave Hettie a complete makeover and turned her into a beauty right before our eyes with her new chin-length bob, super white teeth and minimal makeup. Not to mention that she already had a killer body from doing all that stretching and twisting she was trying to get me and the rest of the residents of Sleepy Hollow to do.

"Not in the least bit happy to see her." I couldn't take my eyes off Jade Lee. Her talons had hooked Jack Henry Ross, sheriff of Sleepy Hollow and my boyfriend, when we were in high school. And it seemed she was trying to hook him now, right there on the sidewalk in front of Higher Grounds Café. "She's the one who came up with my nickname, Creepy Funeral Home Girl, when I was in high school."

It was true. Kids could be so cruel. I was the butt of all their jokes. Granted, growing up in a family business was hard, but mine had to be the funeral home. My granny and parents were also undertakers and we lived in Eternal Slumber Funeral Home. Needless to say, I wasn't the most popular kid in school. Who in the world wanted to have a sleepover in a funeral home? No one. Least of all, Jade Lee Peel, the most popular cheerleader, prom queen and now small town celebrity. Even in high school she had celebrity status thanks to the community. After her mamma died of a stroke, Artie Peel, Jade's father and owner of Artie's Meat and Deli, did everything he could for his daughter, doing her no favors.

All the women in town felt sorry for Jade and

took her under their wing. I blamed the town for blowing up Jade's head as big as the town square.

"That's right." Hettie patted me on the back. "Your class reunion is this weekend."

"Yep." It was the only word I could muster up. My heart was breaking watching Jade and Jack exchange smiles, giggles, and whatever other else line of bull malarkey she was feeding him. No doubt trying to reel my handsome boyfriend into her lair.

Jade and Jack, their names were synonymous in high school. They even had their own nickname like Brangelina. JJ. Thinking about them with their own combined name made my stomach hurt and the feelings of the past flooded right back as if ten years had never passed. Only now I couldn't run over to my bedroom in the funeral home, slam my door and bury my head in the pillow.

"And you were in charge of the reunion, right?" Hettie reminded me.

I admit I almost didn't send Jade an invitation, but my good ole Southern manners, like Granny called it, won out. I can't say I didn't have a daydream about Jade coming back to town and seeing me in Jack's arms, but I certainly didn't daydream the other way around. I wasn't even on the high school reunion committee in high school, but the school called me since I lived here and asked me to put it together. Like Granny said, people were living longer, making funerals a little sparse. I had nothing better to do.

A white van with sketchy windows came plowing down the street and abruptly stopped right next to Jade and Jack. A bunch of men jumped out holding a big boom microphone and camera equipment.

Jade grabbed Jack by the arm and smiled as big as the day was long.

"Smile, Jack." I read her lips and heard her Southern twang in my head.

Jack fluffed up like a bandy rooster, sticking his chest out for all the world to see his sheriff's badge. The cameraman walked around them with the camera on his shoulder, taking shots from all angles.

"Yoo-hoo! Jade! Remember me?" Beulah waved and patted her chest. "Beulah Paige Bellefry! You used to play with these pearls in my Sunday school class." Beulah's grin took up her entire face. The balls of her cheeks squished up into her eyes.

Jade planted that sweet, fake smile across her face, giving Beulah a hug. Both of Jade's hands planted on the tops of Beulah's shoulders, giving her a pat on the left and then a pat on the right.

Jade's eyes grazed the grass along the town square, which drew them up to the gazebo. Our eyes caught. An easy smile was planted at the corners of her mouth. I glared at her, finding it almost impossible not to return her disarming smile.

She threw her keys to a young girl standing behind her. The girl ran in front of Jade and pulled open the door to the café, cowering down behind it. Her long brown hair was flat to her head. She had brown doe eyes and an olive complexion. She wore large black-rimmed glasses that were entirely too big for her face. But who was I to judge. I was by far no fashion expert. But it wasn't a surprise Jade surrounded herself with people who weren't as pleasing to the eye as she was. She always liked being the pretty one, center of attention.

I watched in horror as Jade grabbed Beulah's hand and tucked her other in the crook of Jack Henry's arm, dragging them both inside Higher Grounds. My heart sunk. My knees buckled. And any sort of Southern manners I had were thrown out the window.

"How do I look?" I ran my hand over my hair.

"Greasy." Hettie Bell's nose ruffled. She was never one to sugarcoat nothing.

I turned to Granny.

"Emma Lee, you are smarter than her. If dumb was dirt, she'd only cover about half an acre." Granny had her own way of trying to make me feel better.

I wasn't sure if she had just insulted me or had

given me a compliment. My head tilted, my eyes lowered and I stared at her.

"You are beautiful inside and out." Mable Claire jingled her way over. Mable Claire kept a lot of change in her pockets. She gave out dimes here and there to people who she passed on the street. "It's early, honey."

"Stop it." Hettie stepped up. "You are in workout clothes. She's gonna know you've been working out." Hettie jabbed my shoulder with her finger. "You are not the creepy funeral girl anymore. You are an important member of this town."

She was right. I wasn't that girl anymore and I had Jack Henry Ross now.

Granny scooted closer. She bent her lips to my ear. She smelled of cinnamon and sugar, easing my belly pain somewhat. She whispered, "Emma Lee, you go on in there and get your man."

I pulled back and we held each other's eyes for a second. I straightened my shoulders and stomped my way across the square and stood right in front of Higher Grounds.

I looked in the front window. Everyone inside was making a fuss over Jade Lee Peel being back in town, Ms. Sleepy Hollow herself, and everyone acted as if it were Christmas day. They were all crowded around her. Even little children who didn't know her, but knew of her and her legacy.